Dreaming The Moon

Izzy Robertson

This is a First Edition of the paperback
Dreaming The Moon:
Good magic, dark forces, faeries, goblins & an ordinary girl
Copyright © February 2015 Izzy Robertson
ISBN: 978-1-910094-13-6
eBook ISBN: 978-1-910094-14-3
Published February 2015
By Magic Oxygen
www.MagicOxygen.co.uk
editor@MagicOxygen.co.uk

Izzy Robertson has asserted her right under the Copyright, Designs and Patents Act 1988 to be identified as the author of this work.

Edited by Simon West

A catalogue record for this book is available from
the British Library

All characters appearing in this work are fictitious. Any resemblance to real persons, living or dead, is purely coincidental.

All rights reserved. This publication is not included under licences issued by the Copyright Agency. No part of this publication may be used other than for the purpose for which it is intended nor may any part be reproduced or transmitted, in any form or by any means, electronically or mechanically, including photocopying, recording or any storage or retrieval system without prior written permission from the publisher.

Requests for permission should be addressed to:-
The Editor, Magic Oxygen
editor@MagicOxygen.co.uk

Printed by Lightning Source UK Ltd; committed to improving environmental performance by driving down emissions and reducing, reusing and recycling waste.

View their eco-policy at www.LightningSource.com

Set in 11.5pt Times New Roman
Headings set in Cornish

Also by Izzy Robertson

When Joe Met Alice

Catching Up With The Past

Dedication

Brian, Jed and Zack
always

Betty Robertson
miss you every day

Sophie Graves and Anne Maloney
for telling me I could and believing that I would

Thank You

Brian Robertson
for endless patience and cups of tea

Tracey and Simon West at Magic Oxygen
this wouldn't have happened without you

Alex Smith of GraphicAlex.co.uk
for photographic inspiration

Jenny Dixon, Anne Maloney and Lucy West.
the wonderful souls who read and gave feedback in the early stages

Jed and Zack Robertson
for musical information and inspiration

Chapter 1

R**OBYN** Greening awoke with her heart racing and a clawing sense of panic following her up through the syrupy layers of sleep. Abruptly throwing off her duvet, she searched through her foggy brain for the source. "Late, late for an exam," her mind screamed. "They're after you," something else shouted over the top. Robyn shot out of bed and was halfway across the room when reality caught up with her. She slumped thankfully in the chair by her desk and took a deep breath, feeling her heart rate slow as relief washed over her. Exams were over, they had been for a week. She was officially free.

Knowing that it was pointless going back to bed, Robyn padded down to the kitchen. Her mother was there having breakfast before she went to work.

"Hi, honey, you're up early."

Robyn topped up the teapot and poured fresh mugs for both of them. She joined her mother at the table. "Had one of those dreams again," she said. "They're starting to drive me nuts."

Her mum looked at her sympathetically. "Still running to get to an exam on time?"

Robyn shrugged. "Running to get somewhere. It's dark and I'm late and I can't seem to get where I'm going. I would've thought it'd have stopped by now."

"A-levels are a big thing, hon, and I know how nervous you were, even though you've worked so hard. It'll settle down."

"Hmm," Robyn sighed. "I wish it would hurry up. I'd really like a lie in."

Her mother laughed and stood up. "It will, I promise." She ruffled Robyn's hair as she passed. "Trust me, I'm a psychologist."

Robyn followed her into the hall. "Have a good day," she said

"Thanks, you too. You meeting up with Ant today?"

"No," Robyn sighed. Ant was her boyfriend of seven months. "He's working, then he's out with the boys tonight. We're going out tomorrow but I might pop down and see him for a coffee when he finishes. He goes away next week for a fortnight and then obviously I'm away most of August. Got to make the most of him while I can."

"Well, have fun, and try and relax a bit. You deserve it you know."

Robyn did try but she had come to the conclusion that she wasn't very good at relaxing. She read for a while, listened to some music and half-heartedly tried to get some things ready for her month away. In the end she gave up, and sat by her bedroom window gazing listlessly out into the garden. The weather seemed to echo her mood. It was unforgivingly hot and the sky was a bleached blue, as if the effort of staying up there in the heat had sapped it dry. The heaviness was almost unbearable, but Robyn knew some of that lay in her heart.

"Oh, Ant," she sighed. "I'm going to miss you so much." The thought of seven weeks apart drove her crazy and again she rued her promise to Julianne to come and help her in the shop during August. Even if it was one of her favourite places to be.

Julianne ran what was often referred to in a mocking and derogatory way as a New Age shop. Robyn had never been able to understand why people laughed at places like that. She had always found them to be little havens of peace and stillness in the hurly burly of life, and The Dragon's Rest was the best of them all. It was in a small village on the North Cornish coast, a little further up than Newquay, an area that her parents loved. Robyn knew that her Mum and Dad had been there on several holidays before she had come along and she could understand why. It was quiet, despite the tourists, and there was a sense of oldness and wildness that was hard to put into words but that she could feel in her bones.

Over the past few years, when they had been staying there in the summer, she had spent so much time in the shop with Julianne that she had laughingly been called their spare hand. Julianne had offered her a proper official summer job for this year and Robyn had jumped at the chance. That had been before she met Ant, before she had tumbled head over heels. But it was too late to do anything about it now. And besides, Ant had said he would come down and see her.

Robyn gave up trying to relax after lunch. She took the bus into town and met up with her friend Cara for some window shopping. Cara favoured high street fashion, while Robyn's style was more eclectic, a kind of charity shop come back end of town boutique rock Goth mix. Cara's clothing featured all colours of the rainbow; Robyn's was black with the occasional bit of purple sneaking in. Robyn often thought when she caught sight of them in a mirror that they were light and darkness personified, but they had been friends for so long that they both saw beyond the clothes. Sometimes Robyn thought that Cara knew her better than she knew herself.

"So," Cara said as they flopped down in a coffee shop after two gleeful hours of trying on outfits and shoes. "What's up?"

"Who says anything's up," Robyn countered.

Cara grinned but her eyes were serious. "I can read you like a book, missy, I know when something's up. Spill."

Robyn sighed. "It's nothing really. Just that I'm going to miss Ant this summer. And I know we're going out tomorrow but I so want to see him today as well. I'm just being pathetic and needy but… but he's out tonight with his football buddies."

"Ah, love, the treacherous beast," Cara said sympathetically. "Nothing pathetic about that. So why are you with me and not with him now then?"

"He's working. Plus you know how he likes to organise his time."

"So organise time. Text him and meet him after work for half an hour. Then you'll see him and you won't be cutting in on his "boy" time. Or," Cara leaned forward conspiratorially "you could always just turn up and surprise him."

"Don't know if he'd like that."

"For heaven's sake, Robyn, you're the love of his life. Of course he'll like it." Cara was insistent but Robyn was still looking dubious. "Text him then."

"He'll say no."

"He does and he's an eejit. Robyn look, you just want to see him quickly, it's not like you're going to steal his evening. It's no big deal. Why are you so worried about it? Has he been dictatorial again?"

Robyn sighed. She knew Cara found Ant difficult at times. She could understand why, but Cara didn't know him like she did. She shook her head. "No, it's just… you know he doesn't like surprises."

"Yes, but everything's not always about him, is it?" Cara asked pointedly. "Sometimes, ooh, just that once in a blue moon, you are allowed to put yourself first. So. You just turn up, have a quick snog, and then you both go home, he goes out with his mates and I come over to yours for a soppy film and a chocolate fest."

Robyn giggled despite her unease. Cara always made her laugh. "Sounds like a plan."

"Sorted." Cara drained the last of her coffee and checked her watch. "I've got to go, need to do a couple of things before I come over. See you about half seven, eightish?"

"Great," said Robyn, waving her friend out of the door. She stirred the froth at the bottom of her cup, absentmindedly spooning it into her mouth as she surveyed the passersby outside the window. Why was she making such a big thing out of dropping by to see Ant? It wasn't as if she'd never done it before. It was just that Ant was a very private, very organised person. He liked everything to be pre-organised, no surprises, no spur of the minute ideas. Robyn often wondered why he was with her, since she was the opposite, as chaotic as it was possible to be. Maybe opposites did attract to balance each other, but she had noticed over the exams that he had become much more of a stickler for time and planning. She had respected that, given him room to study, but even now the exams were over he was still edgy.

"Well," she thought. "I'm still having weird stress dreams so maybe it's not that surprising." She touched the silver heart that hung on a fine chain round her neck, his gift to her for her eighteenth birthday five weeks before.

"It's mine," he'd said. "And now it's yours."

Robyn rose and left the cafe, mindful that it was almost half past five, and Ant would be finishing work. But halfway down the pedestrian precinct she hesitated, stopping by the seats a short distance away from the shop where he worked. Her pulse was beginning to accelerate. When she had first started seeing Ant her heart would dance with nerves and excitement whenever she saw him. Now though, there was less of the tingle and more of the nerves because she never knew how he would react to her, especially appearing without warning. How, she wondered, could one person have this much effect on another? And why did she feel that she was doing something wrong? She stayed where she was, deciding that he probably wouldn't want her to come into the store.

She'd catch him on his way out.

Robyn watched most of the employees leave. Ant was almost the last, excepting the managers, but he came out chatting to a blonde girl who she recognised from the many football matches that she had been at to cheer Ant on. She was just about to walk over to them when the blonde turned and put her hands on Ant's chest. Robyn froze, waiting for Ant to push the girl away but instead he picked her up and swung her round. By the time he put her down their laughter had become a kiss and Robyn's blood had turned to ice. It was a good two minutes before she managed to make herself move and they still hadn't come up for air.

Robyn turned to walk away but found she couldn't. She didn't relish confrontation but a sudden fury enveloped her. She strode over to them.

"Hello Ant," she said quietly.

Had it been under different circumstances, she would have laughed at the way they shot apart as though they had both been electrocuted. But it just wasn't funny.

"Robyn, hi, I was just... this is..." Ant stuttered.

"I could see very well what you were doing and I know who she is," Robyn said coldly. "Is there something you'd like to tell me?" She glared at him.

"What are you doing here anyway?" Ant said, gaining some composure. "You're not supposed to..."

"What? Be here? It's a public street, Anthony, in case you hadn't noticed and I just wanted to say hi before," she cast the girl a scathing glance, "your night out with the boys."

"But I told you..."

"I know what you told me. So many things that you've told me. It's what you haven't told me that I'm worried about." She looked over at the girl again. "How long, Ant? How long have you been lying to me?"

"You said you were going to tell her," piped up the girl.

Ant turned to her crossly. "How could I? We had exams and it was her birthday. How could I?"

"Oh for goodness" sake, Ant, I'm not some china doll," Robyn said, although that was very much how she did feel. "Give me some credit. And tell me how long you've been seeing her."

Ant looked at her, cornered. "Since Easter," he mumbled.

The bottom fell out of Robyn's world then, but she was damned if she was going to let them see it. She pulled herself up to her full five foot five and took a deep breath.

"Well, I guess you deserve each other then. I'll leave you to it. Here." She reached up and tore the heart necklace from her throat, tossing it at Ant. It fell on the ground and he had to grovel to pick it up. "Not sure why you gave this to me. Best pass it on to her, eh? I'm sure she'll look after it. Although," she turned and faced the girl, "I'd be wary of it if I were you. It's a slippery little devil."

She turned on her heel and marched away.

"Robyn," she heard Ant call after her.

"Don't bother," she yelled without turning back. "And don't phone me either."

Robyn walked fast to the furthest bus stop she could from the town centre. If the bus hadn't pulled in just as she got there she would have kept going. She needed to keep moving, to get as far as she could from Ant and the girl. She climbed on and found the seat furthest away from everyone that she could. Then she sat, staring mindlessly out of the window, seeing nothing except betrayal and hurt. She didn't even notice as the tears began to run down her face.

She managed to gather herself together a little on the short walk home, trying to muster some anger and righteous outrage, but as soon as her mother saw her and drew her into a hug with a worried "Sweetheart, what on earth is wrong?', the tears started again and this time she knew they would never stop. Her explanation was sobbed out in fits and starts, while her mum stroked her hair and her dad, who came in part way through, made cups of tea and then sat holding her hand. Eventually, when she was all cried out, her parents began to talk gently, saying the things she needed to hear but couldn't believe. How she deserved better, how she would find better, someone who would be true, how time would heal her heart even though it felt as though it would never be anything but broken.

"I'm going to phone Mark," her dad said, getting up. "Cancel our dinner tonight."

Her mother nodded, but Robyn shook her head. "No, you mustn't. You haven't seen them for ages."

"Honey, we're not leaving you feeling like this," he insisted.

"I'll be OK, honestly," Robyn said in a voice that was still shaking slightly. "Don't think I've got any tears left. Anyway, Cara's coming over later so I won't be on my own."

"It doesn't feel right, going out when you've just had such a shock." That was her mother. "I still can't believe he would do that."

"Well, he did." Robyn felt a flicker of anger. Not pleasant, but it was better than despair. "And I don't want him to be the reason you miss your night out. He may have wrecked my evening but he's not going to ruin yours as well."

Her father grinned at her mother. "Now where does she get that steely determination from?" he mused. Her mother batted at him lightly with the back of her hand.

"Cheek," she growled.

Robyn couldn't help smiling. Her parents had a great line in banter. Her mum smiled at her, stroked her cheek. "Brave girl," she said.

"Please go out," Robyn said. "Really, I'll be OK."

Her parents exchanged a look. "OK," her mother said finally, "but not 'til Cara gets here." Robyn was about to argue but her father held up his hand.

"Sounds fair to me."

"But you'll be late. She may not get here 'til eight." Robyn was starting to feel upset again.

"That's fine," Mum said.

"I could phone her, ask her to come earlier." Robyn fought off the tears that were threatening to well over.

"Sweetheart, you don't look like you want to be phoning anyone. I'll call her, OK? You go and have a nice hot shower, and we'll get ready, and then we'll see what happens."

Chapter 2

WHEN Robyn came back down half an hour later, having let the shower wash away another flood of tears, her parents were ready to go.

"Cara will be here in a few minutes," her Mum said. "And I think it's a good thing Anthony is nowhere in the vicinity. She sounded ready to rip his head off."

Robyn and her father both let out a laugh. Cara was tiny and gorgeous in a very ethereal way. With her fair, fair hair and her small, slender figure, she looked as though a puff of wind would blow her over. But she certainly did not suffer fools gladly and was a formidable adversary whether in sport or with words. Few people at school had ever had the nerve to argue with Cara.

When Cara swept in shortly before eight and gave her the biggest hug, she nearly lost it again, somehow managing to keep her tears at bay until she had waved goodbye to her parents. Then she followed her friend into the kitchen, where Cara was busy unloading one of the bags she had brought.

"You moving in?" Robyn joked half-heartedly.

"No, but your Mum said I could stay over. In return for making you eat something." She bustled over and put the oven on. "So we're having pizza, and then I have the comfort package – cherry cookie ice cream, wine and," she picked it up and waved it at Robyn, "an industrial sized bar of chocolate. Oh, and a selection of films ranging from the sublime to the ridiculous. Can you find us some glasses? I'll just get the pizza in and you can tell me what happened with that filthy swine of an Anthony."

Robyn got out two wine glasses and poured. She sat at the table next to her best friend, tried to speak and started to cry again.

Eventually, over pizza and ice cream the whole story came out. And through her tears, Robyn couldn't help smiling as Cara used every expletive under the sun and explained in detail what she would like to do to a certain part of Anthony's anatomy with a rusty knife and no anaesthetic.

"He's a low life scumbucket," Cara pronounced eventually, when they had finished the ice cream. She topped up their glasses and they took the wine and chocolate into the sitting room. "And she's a low life scumbag too, but not as low life as him. He's lower than low life."

"Is that possible?" Robyn enquired.

"It is most certainly possible – he, unfortunately, is living proof. He is also the biggest idiot on the planet. All those headers must have turned his brains to mush."

Robyn tried to smile, but the memory of how Ant would look at her when he came off the pitch, as if she was the only person there, the only person in the world, sent a bolt through her heart. Cara could see it, because she reached over and squeezed Robyn's hand.

"You deserve so much better. I know how you feel about him but he wasn't always easy to be with, was he? Quite manipulative sometimes? Liked to get his own way?"

Robyn opened her mouth to defend Ant, then shut it again. Cara wasn't wrong. In fact, she was very far from wrong. Much as Robyn didn't want to admit it, Ant did have a manipulative and narcissistic streak.

"You may still feel in love with him," Cara continued, "but he is not worthy of you. He's not even worth your toe nail clippings."

"Eeuw!" Robyn exclaimed, but her friend was in full swing.

"I hereby declare that the imbecile known as Anthony Langman is deemed unworthy by me, the high priestess of the temple of Robynity, and will no longer be permitted to worship at the feet of her High and Mighty Fairy Queen Robyn. He will be banished forthwith from the land of Robyness and shall spend the rest of his sorry days wandering the wasteland with his floozy and eating," she hesitated, "only cabbages and slugs. Raw."

Robyn sucked in a breath and then let out a guffaw. The next thing they knew, they were both rolling around with laughter, unable to contain themselves. But Robyn's laughter was brittle and Cara knew it. She hugged her friend, desperately trying to make it better.

"I'm so glad you're here," Robyn choked.

By the time Robyn's parents returned, the two girls had ridden the whole emotional rollercoaster, and after a cup of hot chocolate they all headed up to bed. Robyn was grateful that Cara had stayed; her friend's quiet breathing was an anchor in the lonely dark sea of the night. She herself slept fitfully, haunted by dreams where she was lost and searching desperately to find her way, to find... something. In the morning she was still exhausted.

"I think you're psychic," Cara said.

"Yeah, right."

"No, seriously." Cara propped herself up on one arm. "You've been having these dreams for a while, haven't you, and we put it down to the exams. But maybe you were picking up something else. You know. Like an early scumbucket warning system."

Robyn was highly doubtful but she couldn't completely dismiss the idea. The timing was right for starters.

"Right, missy." Cara bounced out of her sleeping bag. "Get moving before that sombre look takes hold. You and I are going out to have some fun today."

"I want to get my hair cut," Robyn said, "and before you accuse me of committing a breakup cliché, I've wanted to get it cut for ages. The only reason I didn't was because he liked it long, and that's no longer a factor."

They discussed their plans over breakfast. Robyn's mother was all for her having a new look. "Have a great time. See you later."

They headed out and got the bus into town. Cara was busy texting while Robyn sat back and watched the houses and cars go by. She didn't know whether to feel upset, angry or relieved that Ant hadn't bothered to even try and contact her.

"Yes!" Cara exclaimed, checking a text that has just come in.

"What?" It had shaken Robyn out of her stupor.

Cara was grinning madly. "Never mind. You'll see later. Just a little surprise, is all."

"Hmm. It always makes me nervous when you look that pleased with yourself."

They alighted at the top end of town and wandered through the little arcades of bohemian and vintage shops. Robyn stopped outside a no appointment walk in hair salon but Cara tugged her over to look at some boots in the window opposite.

"Hey. I want to get my hair done," Robyn protested, but Cara pulled her into the shop.

"Later. You have to try on this skirt."

Much as she hated to admit it, Cara was right. She left with the skirt, a black and purple knee length net and velvet creation, and a long sleeved black top.

"I am so bad," she said.

"No," Cara demurred. "You're being nice to yourself with a little retail therapy."

"Right. Hair now."

"Wait." Cara looked at her watch. "No. We have to be somewhere in ten minutes."

"What? Where?"

"That surprise I mentioned. Don't look so panicky, it's a nice one, I promise."

"Cara," Robyn began, then gave up, realising that she had no option but to follow her friend or be abandoned. Cara ducked and weaved through the shoppers and the wanderers and finally came to a halt outside a small glass fronted building. Robyn stared. It was a hair salon, but not just any one.

"I'll never get an appointment here," she said. "They're booked up months in advance."

"Aha," Cara said. "Usually yes. But when your fairy godmother," she performed a theatrical bow "is the daughter of the owner's best friend, there is often a way. Come on." She opened the door and virtually shoved Robyn through it.

"Cara. How lovely to see you." The elegant dark haired woman behind the desk rose and came round to kiss Cara's cheek. "You survived the exams then. How did it go?"

"OK I think, thanks Eleanor," Cara replied. "And thanks so much for fitting us in. This is Robyn."

"It's nice to meet you, Robyn," Eleanor said, extending her hand. "And so sorry to hear about your rotten day yesterday. He must be a fool. Still, we'll make him realise what a mistake he's made." She lifted a strand of Robyn's long black hair and rubbed her hands together with glee. "Let's go and have some fun."

"I'm off to get donuts," Cara said. "Back in a bit."

Eleanor led Robyn through the salon and sat her down near the back. They both looked at her reflection in the mirror and Robyn was suddenly very aware of how pale she was and how red rimmed her eyes were, despite the heavy black eyeliner.

"So," Eleanor said gently. "What did you have in mind?"

Robyn took a deep breath, staring at the hair that nearly reached her waist. "I want it all cut off. Up to here," she added, indicating just below her jawline. Eleanor looked slightly taken aback.

"That's a big change," she commented. "Are you sure? Now may not be the best time to make a radical decision like that."

Robyn met her eyes in the mirror. "Really, I'm sure. I've been wanting to do it since last summer, but I never got round to it and then I met... him, and he liked it long, so I didn't, but now..." She paused. "Now I can please myself."

"Well, OK." Eleanor still sounded doubtful. "Do you know exactly what you'd like me to do?" And as Robyn described what she wanted, she could see the sparkle in Eleanor's eye and the smile dancing over her face. When Cara got back with the donuts, Eleanor was well into the cut.

"Wow," Cara said as the long strands of hair hit the floor. "This is going to be amazing."

"You have no idea," said Eleanor.

When it was finished, they all gazed at Robyn's reflection. Her hair now fell in a chin length bob, sharp and precise, the jet black overlaid with a deep jewel purple.

"Totally amazing," Cara confirmed.

"It's fantastic," Robyn whispered. "Thank you so much." She felt tears welling up again. "Just perfect."

Eleanor smiled. "You look gorgeous."

"Very elfin," Cara said. "Even if you aren't blonde."

"Are elves always blonde?" Eleanor asked with a grin. Cara shrugged and waggled a strand of her own hair.

"Who knows? Never met one," she said. "Maybe I'm just being blondist."

When they left the salon, Robyn felt strange but elated. She had no long curtain to hide behind now, and that was oddly liberating. She handed Cara her mobile.

"Take a picture please."

"Bet I know where this is going."

Robyn sent the picture to Ant immediately along with the words "Your loss." Then she blocked him from her phone.

Robyn felt almost euphoric for the rest of the afternoon, but her mood crashed that evening and she found herself restless and weepy over the next couple of days. Although she had blocked Ant from her phone, she was angry and upset that he hadn't even tried to contact her some other way. Soon she had made a decision.

"I'm going to phone Julianne and see if I can go down early," she told her parents. "You don't mind, do you? I'm driving myself crazy here on my own."

Chapter 3

ON Thursday afternoon, Julianne met Robyn at the train station. "So glad to see you, my lovely," she said, enveloping Robyn in a huge hug. "Love the hair. Now let's get your things into the car and you can tell me everything."

Being with Julianne always made Robyn feel lifted and telling her sorry tale again wasn't quite as bad as she'd thought. Julianne tutted and tsked appropriately and by the time they got to the Dragon's Rest, Robyn was feeling better than she had in days. Julianne pulled the car into the driveway that ran up the side of the shop.

"It's all ready for you," she said.

Robyn shouldered her backpack and lifted her suitcase out of the boot, while Julianne opened the kitchen door. She handed Robyn the key.

"All yours, sweetie. Now go on in and get settled and I'll make us a cup of tea. And later when we've closed up, Jim and I are taking you to The Anchor for dinner."

Robyn looked at her friend, a wave of affection and gratitude almost overcoming her.

"Thanks so much J," she said. "I can't tell you how much this..."

"It's OK." Julianne's voice was gentle. "Really."

Robyn stepped through the door into the kitchen diner which ran the width of the narrow building. Crossing to the other side, she turned left into the hallway. It housed a corridor which ran forward into what was the shop store room, and a flight of stairs which ran up to the bedsit above the shop.

Her bedsit. At least for the next seven weeks.

Upstairs, she put her luggage down and turned slowly, surveying the room. At the street end were large windows through which the sun was pouring. There was a low coffee table with a big sofa and an arm chair. A two tier cabinet stood in the corner holding a small TV and a sound system. There were several mismatched bookcases lining the walls. The bed was further back in the room, a small table beside it. A chest of drawers and a wooden wardrobe stood in an alcove formed by the bathroom wall at the back of the room. A smile crept across Robyn's face. It was perfect.

By the time Julianne came up with the tea, Robyn had put her clothes away and was arranging some of her other bits and pieces.

"You look right at home," Julianne observed.

"I feel at home," Robyn agreed. "I've always loved it up here."

Once they had finished their tea, they headed down into the shop to see Jim, who swept Robyn up in another bear hug and almost danced her round the shop, making their customers laugh.

"Put her down, for goodness sake," Julianne mock-scolded.

"It's exceptionally good to see you," Jim said, as he finally obeyed. "We're so glad you still wanted to come."

"Wild dragons wouldn't have kept me away." Robyn looked fondly at the pair. Jim and Julianne were in their mid fifties, he tall, sharp and angular with a grey plait that hung down his back, she petite and plumply curvaceous. Whenever Robyn heard the words Mother Earth, Julianne was the first person that came to mind.

"A little gremlin tells me you've spent the last few days on the metaphorical battlefield," Jim continued, while Julianne poked her tongue out at him.

"Yes, well, I guess they're not all knights in shining armour," Robyn sighed. "I picked a frog. Now I have to deal with the consequences."

"You're in magical country now," Julianne added. "Maybe that will help. And the frog will get his comeuppance soon enough, I have no doubt. They always do."

"All hail the wise one," Jim said. Julianne raised her eyebrows and pointed at him.

"They always do," she repeated meaningfully.

They closed the shop at half past six and walked over to The Anchor. Over dinner, Robyn caught up with the comings and goings of the village and its inhabitants since the previous year.

"How's it going this summer?" she asked, meaning the shop.

"It's been OK, patchy but OK," Julianne replied. "The weather's been quite unpredictable, sudden rainstorms out of the blue which have sent people in to us. But I don't know, it all feels sort of unsettled."

"It'll be fine," Jim said positively. Robyn almost missed the warning glance he shot Julianne. Almost. But before she could question him about it, Julianne spotted Fiona, a local artist that Robyn had become very friendly with the year before, and called her over to join them. By the time Robyn fell into bed that night it was past midnight, and she was exhausted. She curled up under the duvet and dropped into a deep sleep.

It was dark – intensely, terrifyingly dark. The barest sliver of a new moon illuminated a mercurial thread of sea in the distance, but where she stood the blackness was total and heavily oppressive. Just moving through it was like walking through treacle. She stumbled forward, desperately trying to see something, anything. A branch caught her arm, making her jump, and she stumbled again, feeling her way but not seeming to get anywhere. Eventually she stopped and looked around again, desperately straining her eyes to pick out something familiar, some outline or shape. But she could see nothing except for the narrow ribbon of sea far ahead of her, hear nothing except her own ragged breath. Everything around her was perfectly and absolutely still. She tried again to move, slowly easing her way toward the silvered water, concentrating hard so as not to lose her footing in the inky darkness. And despite the silence, the stillness, the sense of isolation, she was acutely aware that someone or something was watching her.

Robyn awoke with her pulse hammering and the feeling that she was still being observed. She sat up, taking in her surroundings. The early sun was curling round the edges of the curtains and falling in gentle lines across the carpet. The furniture looked solid and comforting. Overhead she could hear gulls shrieking and squabbling.

"Phew," she thought. Although it was only half past six, she rose and showered, then headed downstairs. Opening the windows in the kitchen, she took a deep breath of clean air and gently evicted a spider that had got stuck in the sink before she put the kettle on. "You're rather lovely," she told it as she placed it carefully on the window sill. "Go on, you'll be much happier out there than in here." Then, with a cup of tea in hand, she slipped into the shop, planning to reacquaint herself with it before they opened.

No matter how many times Robyn had been in the Dragon's Rest, it never lost its wonder. Coming in from the street, visitors first passed through a small hallway which had been painted a dark grey blue, including the windows. It was lit by strings of fairy lights and had niches and small shelves randomly placed throughout, holding candles, small sculptures and ornaments. On the entrance side there was a cavern set into the wall where a purple dragon lay curled on her nest.

When people then entered the shop itself they were welcomed by the honeyed glow of lamps and the sunlight falling through the high windows running all the way down the right hand side. The shop itself was divided into different areas by clever use of furniture and sections of banister. The main part had tables on two sides and in the centre, plus a few glass display cases, including one which formed part of the counter. There were two subdivisions at the back, one containing books and music, and the other scarves, shawls and a few items of clothing.

Robyn wandered round the tables, relishing the scent of incense that hung in the air. She noticed that there was a semblance of order to the baskets of crystals now. Julianne had them all on one table and labelled. The other tables held a deliciously chaotic mix of ornaments, candle holders, incense burners, wands, stars and many other eclectic and unusual objects. Strings of beads and pendants on chains were suspended from hooks beneath shelves above the tables. From the ceiling hung mobiles, wind chimes and other ornaments, butterflies, stars, dragonflies, which gave the impression of gentle freedom each time a breeze came through the door. She admired the small fairy and dragon pieces that she recognised as Fiona's work and had a look at the new semiprecious jewellery that Julianne had acquired.

Just before eight thirty she put the lights on and lit the incense so that it would be ready when Julianne came in.

"Hey," Julianne greeted her. "You don't hang around, do you?"

Over the morning, Julianne went through everything with her, and they came to an agreement over hours and time off. It wasn't difficult. Robyn was happy to be flexible, and Julianne already knew most of the days that she and/or Jim needed to be away, so it was left as an open arrangement for both sides.

"I'll be here for your first few days," Julianne told her, "and I'm only a phone call away if you need me."

Robyn settled into the rhythm of her summer very quickly, and although the memory of Ant still hung heavy on her heart, she found it easier to lift herself in her new summer life. Although never a morning person, she found she had a new alarm clock in the guise of her dreams, and although they seemed to be growing more intense and frightening with each passing night, she actually enjoyed being up early and having the shop to herself, setting out the incense and candles and standing in the grotto when the coloured lights sprung into life and illuminated the magic. In the first few days she became immersed in the running of the shop, caught up with several friends and spent an evening at Fiona's, talking as the artist worked. Robyn loved to watch Fiona in her workshop, to observe as delicate magical beings appeared from clay or from the tip of her paint brush.

But most of all, Robyn enjoyed the last part of her evenings, when she put on a low lamp in the shop and tidied anything she hadn't done before, ready for the following day. There was just something about the ambience in the room then, a gentle quietness underlain by a sensation, almost a vibration, of something that she couldn't quite place. "Magic," Julianne would call it. "Good energy," would probably be Jim's take. Robyn didn't have an opinion, but whatever it was, it was comforting and exciting in equal measure and she loved it.

"If I ever have a shop," she thought, "it will be just like this."

On the Monday afternoon, Julianne decided that Robyn needed some sunshine and kicked her out after lunch.

"You've worked like a Trojan the last few days," she said. "You deserve some time off."

The sky was as it had been since she'd arrived, a faded scorched blue with dangerous steel clouds threatening a sulky sun. Robyn had a little wander into the other shops just to remind herself of what was there and then headed down the path toward the beach and caves. The village had some unusual features in its landscape, and two beaches. There was easy access to the long sweep of sand at the top from the main street, which was where most of the holiday makers favoured. The other beach was accessed by a path leading away from the bottom end of the road, which ran downwards, parallel to a wide stream that fed from the local river and ended in the sea. By the time it reached the shore, the village was high above to the right, while to the left cave pocked rocks stretched up into towering cliffs. The cliffs were stepped, an odd feature that seemed to be unique to the area, but the caves were the reason most tourists came down here, to see the multiple carvings of labyrinths if they managed to time it right with the tide. The beach itself was a scramble to get to, and stony rather than sand, but Robyn preferred it. It was quieter and much more wild.

As Robyn approached the path she couldn't help but stop and admire the motorbike that was parked at the top. Silver and black, lean and low, it put her in mind of some of the iconic looking bikes she had seen in films.

"Nice," she thought appreciatively.

It was a hot afternoon, the heat shimmering off the ground, the distant sound of the waves repeating like a mantra. Robyn walked slowly, enjoying the breeze and not having to rush, watching some of the visitors scurrying hurriedly down the path, while others scurried back up as if their lives depended on their self imposed time constraints. She liked to notice the little things, the shapes of the windblown trees at the top of the next hill, the strange silvering effect that the sun had on leaves, how the heat seemed to have even slowed the flight of the gulls as they wheeled and swung. Tuning out the buzz of the people around her, she heard music drifting from up ahead.

Rounding the bend, Robyn came upon a scene that almost stopped her in her tracks. On the wooden bridge that forded the stream there stood two young men, buskers, dressed in black jeans and T shirts. They were a striking pair, both tall and slim with long hair. She couldn't help but be reminded of how she and Cara looked together as she watched them. The singer, who was also playing the guitar, had a sandy gold ponytail which reached down below his shoulders. The other man had very dark hair, swinging like a curtain across his face as he moved. He was playing a wooden pipe but there was a bodhran resting near his feet. They looked like a couple of metal heads but that was not the style they were playing. The music was folky but with a hard edge, difficult to place but impossible to ignore. Robyn joined the small crowd that had gathered to listen, taking her shades off to see better.

It was intoxicating. They were playing a ballad, in the real sense of the word and Robyn felt that she could almost have been in any place, in any time. As the notes fell around her the world seemed to slip quietly away, and she was held enthralled. It was a bump coming back to reality when they finished, and she shook her head to clear it before joining in with the applause. She was still standing there slightly dazed as most of the crowd began to move away. The buskers started into a lively reel, and Robyn shook her head again and looked back at them. She found the dark haired man eyeing her up approvingly, the ghost of a grin on his face as he moved his fingers deftly over the pipe. Then he winked at her.

Robyn couldn't help smiling, but she could feel the colour rushing up her cheeks. She put her shades back on and walked quickly away to the beach.

Robyn spent a couple of hours by the sea. The coast was uneven for several miles in either direction. The sea and wind had carved out ledges and plateaus along the cliffs, like some giant hand beginning a sculpture and abandoning it part way through. The rush of the water was mesmeric and just sitting on the rocks with the sun enfolding her, watching the comings and goings from a distance allowed her to finally relax. Although she knew it was impossible, she could still hear faint music but by the time she walked back up along the path they had gone.

Chapter 4

THE following day the fair haired busker came into the shop asking for Julianne.

"She's not in today," Robyn told him. "Can I give her a message?"

"No, it's OK thanks, I'll catch up with her soon." He looked at her appraisingly. "Are you Robyn?"

"Yes," Robyn said, surprised.

A wide smile appeared on his face, lighting him up all the way to his eyes. "It's nice to finally meet you. Julianne talks about you all the time." He held out his hand. "I'm Bryn."

Robyn reached out and took his hand. His grasp was warm and firm.

"Didn't I see you yesterday, walking down to Skells Bay?" Bryn asked.

Robyn coloured slightly. "You were busking with your friend," she answered. "It sounded great. I couldn't get it out of my head all day."

His smile grew even wider. "Hey, if you liked that, you should come and see us when we've got the whole band together. Things get really lively. In fact, we're playing at The Fisherman's on Thursday evening, if you're around."

"Sounds great. If that's what you wanted to tell Julianne, I can pass it on. She's here tomorrow."

A shadow momentarily darkened Bryn's face then he was smiling again. "That'd be great. There is something else but it's not urgent. I'll drop in tomorrow if I can, or catch her on Thursday." He turned to leave, stopping to look back at her. "It was good to meet you, Robyn. Hope I see you again really soon."

Robyn felt the heat rise to her cheeks, but she couldn't stop grinning. "Me too," she thought.

The weather was heavy and oppressive the following day, the blue of the sky almost obscured by steel grey thunder clouds. Julianne seemed on edge, especially after Robyn mentioned Bryn.

"Did he say it was important? Maybe I should call him."

"No, he said it could wait." Robyn was surprised at the urgency in Julianne's voice. "He said he'd catch you today or tomorrow." Julianne seemed unconvinced. "J, what's wrong? You seem really stressed out about something. Come to mention it, Jim seems a bit on the worried side as well. Is this guy causing you problems?" "'cos if he is, I'll tell him where to get off," she finished silently.

"No, no, it's nothing like that," Julianne assured her. "Bryn's lovely. I think you'd get on really well with him. But there's something we've been trying to deal with, and it's not going as well as we'd hoped."

"Can I help?"

Julianne looked at her closely for a long moment. "Perhaps. But it's complicated."

"I can do complicated."

"I know, but there are risks as well. I'd rather keep you away from them. But thank you for the offer, I'll let you know when and if."

"Julianne, you're being very cryptic. What risks? What's happening?" Robyn was intrigued, but Julianne refused to be drawn further.

"Don't worry," she said. "It'll sort itself out one way or the other."

Bryn came in at about half past eleven, and after a quick chat suggested that he and Julianne went and got some lunch.

"If you can spare her."

When they came back, they both looked serious. Robyn finished serving her customer, and then tried to persuade them to tell her what was going on but they would not talk.

"Although," Bryn said cheekily, "maybe I should take you out to lunch too. Don't want you to feel left out."

"Got a sandwich in the kitchen thanks," Robyn joked, but she wouldn't have minded.

"Well, since it's the lunchtime quiet spell I'll go and make us a cup of tea," said Julianne, "and retrieve your sandwich. Pull up a chair," she told Bryn.

So that was how Robyn came to find out that Bryn had grown up in the village and was staying with his parents for the summer, having just finished his second year at university. And that although he was studying marine biology, music played an enormous role in his life.

"I've known them all for years," he said, talking about his band. "Even though we're all over the place now, we try to get together when we can. And the magic still seems to happen, despite the fact that we don't get to rehearse much."

Bryn stayed for another hour or so and then headed off. The shop was busy that afternoon, since the sky was spilling frequent heavy downpours. Robyn and Julianne didn't have much time to talk until they had closed up for the evening. Then they sat in the kitchen with another cup of tea, looking out over the small garden at the back, which was sharply lit by the few rays of sunshine that had managed to break through the clouds.

"That's really eerie light," observed Robyn. "Things always look a bit, I don't know, otherworldly when the light's like this. Look at those hydrangeas. They look as if they're lit from inside."

Julianne had a strange expression on her face. "They do, don't they? They really glow. Who knows, maybe it's not just the light."

Robyn looked at her quizzically.

"Haven't you ever wondered, thought maybe there's something else beyond what we see?" Julianne continued.

"What sort of thing?"

"I don't know, other planes of existence, other beings,"

"What, like angels and aliens and vampires?"

"Yeah, like that. There could be whole worlds out there that we're not aware of."

Robyn gave an involuntary shiver. "You're starting to spook me, J."

Julianne shook her head and seemed to come back to herself. "Sorry, my lovely, I shouldn't be subjecting you to the wild ramblings of my crazed mind. Do you want to come and eat with Jim and me?"

"Thanks but I think I'll stay here. Maybe get an early night."

"OK." Julianne hugged her goodbye. "I'll be in after lunch tomorrow. Then maybe we could all get some dinner and go and see Bryn's band."

Robyn made herself something to eat and took it upstairs to watch a film on the TV. It was gone ten when she went back into the shop for a last tidy. The sky had finally cleared and the moon was out, full and luscious, the light streaming in through the windows. As Robyn moved around she became aware of something, not a sound or a sensation but a steady thrum in the air that she seemed to pick up with some extra sense.

When she stopped to focus on it, it drifted away from her, only to return when she switched her attention to something else.

It was when she stopped by the customer entrance that she noticed the extraordinary effect of the moonlight. Although it flooded in through all the windows that ran the length of the side wall, it seemed to have pooled on the table in the centre of the room that held the baskets of crystals. And while the rest of the shop was in soft indigo shadows, the table seemed to be under a silver stage light that made the crystals sparkle and glitter.

"Oh, wow," Robyn thought, as she was irresistibly drawn over to them. "That's so beautiful."

As she looked over the sea of gems, she couldn't help thinking that any dragon would have been glad to claim it as their hoard. Garnets and amethysts held a fire within them, while moonstones and quartz glimmered with a soft opalescence. The sheen of tiger's eye and goldstone was exquisite. Even the opaque stones such as turquoise and malachite were transformed. As Robyn reached out gently to touch the rose quartz and selenite she felt the thrumming quicken, and this time it seemed to be in her very blood.

She was unaware of how long she stood there, caught up in the moment as she was. It was her foot going to sleep that finally brought her back. The light had shifted a little, and the effect had faded, but she could still feel that little pulse of wonder as she touched the stones. When Robyn finally went to bed that night it was past midnight, and she tumbled quickly into dreams.

It was dark, as always, thick blackness only broken in the distance by moonlight on the sea. The familiar feeling of panic began to rise in her chest as she tried to fight her way forward, this time keeping her eyes firmly focused on that tiny scrap of silver. It seemed even harder to get anywhere this time, and she was far more aware of being watched, not just by one but by many pairs of eyes. She fought hard not to allow the fear to overcome her completely and turn her feet to stone, continuing to drag one in front of the other even though she just wanted to scream. She plunged her hands into her pockets, hoping against hope that she might find a torch or some matches, but her pockets held only crystals. "He wants them," whispery voices hissed around her. "Give them to him."

Robyn woke yet again in a tangle of bed sheets, her heart pounding painfully against her ribcage. "This is getting ridiculous," she muttered as the room came into focus and she realised she was safe. She was on edge that morning. She was finding it harder by the day to shake the dreams off. Rather than being left with a faint sense of unease, she could now remember them in terrifying detail. And although they were dreams, they were always so similar and so intense that she couldn't help but feel that there was something else to them, some truth she couldn't quite grasp. Despite being busy in the shop that morning, she couldn't lift the shadow hanging on her and was still listless and jumpy when Julianne arrived in the afternoon.

"You look shattered," Julianne observed.

"Didn't sleep very well last night. Bad dream," Robyn told her. She continued to pace round the shop, rearranging the stock and then de-rearranging it.

"Take a break and get some air," Julianne said after an hour. "You're making me antsy as well."

Robyn did feel better outside. She took a walk across the fields to the woods at the top of the village, enjoying the peace and quiet, the lazy hum of insects, the dappled light on the path that moved gently with the leaves. It was true English woodland, oak and beech, ash and birch, the massive old trees interspersed with the younger willowy ones. She wandered in as far as the ancient oak that rose above all the others and had the most enormous trunk that bifurcated part way up, the two parts twining round each other as they reached skyward. Robyn could never stop herself from stroking the rough bark, wondering about all the things that it must have witnessed.

She was on her way back when she saw the creature, moving through the trees to her left. It was a dog, but it didn't seem to be attached to an owner. As she continued she realised that it was keeping pace with her and edging gradually closer. Warning hairs stood up on her arms, an unpleasant tingle of danger that made her breathing rate increase. She sped up a little, but so did the dog. It was close enough now for her to see just how big it was, at least the size of a Great Dane, but completely black with a thick shaggy coat. She couldn't identify the breed but she had never seen anything like it before. Its eyes were the thing that freaked her out most. They were red and they were focused totally on her.

"Stay calm. Think," Robyn told herself. She could see the edge of the woods now and the field beyond. She continued to walk rapidly until she was about twenty metres from the tree line. Then she ran.

Robyn had never been much of an athlete; Cara had pretty much left her standing any time they had been put up against one another. But somehow the fear and adrenaline gave her a real boost. She was aware that the dog accelerated a split second after she did but she was half way across the field by the time she realised that it was no longer following her.

Robyn stood doubled over trying to get her breath back. She looked back to see the dog standing at the edge of the trees, watching her. It stayed there until she began to move again, then it melted back into the shadows. Robyn was glad to be back in the sunshine, but the warmth did little to stop the shivers that the dog had given her. It struck her as unusual since she loved dogs, even the biggest ones, and they seemed to react positively to her.

"But there always has to be a rogue," she thought.

She was half way up the High Street when she noticed Bryn with his busker friend and a couple of other guys outside the pub, unloading equipment from the back of a blue van. Bryn looked up and saw her. She raised her hand but he said something to the others and crossed the road to speak to her.

"That looks heavy," she said.

He laughed. "Yes, but at least it's exercise. Saves me a fortune in gym fees. So, you guys are still coming tonight?"

Robyn nodded. "Wouldn't miss it."

"See you later then. I'd better go before I get accused of skiving."

Robyn was in a better mood by the time she got back to work, but the faint sense of unease remained, an annoying tickle in the back of her head. She did her best to keep busy for the rest of the afternoon, alphabetising the books and trying to ignore the odd things that had happened. She could feel Julianne watching her, but wanted to avoid giving her a chance to ask questions.

It was with a jump that she finally realised Julianne was closing up for the evening. Hurriedly she put the last few books on the bookshelf and half ran back into the shop. Too fast. She caught the corner of the crystals table as she flew past and it tilted and bucked. She managed to stop it going over completely, but half the baskets had fallen, spilling their contents everywhere.

"Oh no." She looked at Julianne in horror. "I'm so sorry. I'm such a klutz. Don't worry, I'll clear up."

"It's fine, really," Julianne said comfortingly, but Robyn was already on the floor, setting the baskets the right way up. "Accidents happen. We'll clear it up together. It doesn't surprise me that something gave. You've been so stressed all day I was kind of expecting an explosion of some sort."

"Sorry," Robyn muttered again.

Julianne squatted next to her and began to pick up crystals. "So. You want to tell me what's got you so uptight?"

Robyn was silent for a moment. "It's stupid, really," she said. "It's just... I've been having bad dreams for months and it's always the same. I thought it was because of the exams, you know, but they're long finished. And the dreams are getting worse. I can remember them so clearly now where I couldn't before and they seem so real. I wake up in a panic every morning. It's horrible."

"What do you dream?"

"It's pitch black, all I can see is moonlight on the sea, and I'm trying to get somewhere or find something but I can hardly move and I know there's something watching me. Damn, that sounds pathetic. The curse of an overactive imagination, huh?"

"It sounds scary. Do you know what you're looking for?"

"Not a clue," said Robyn, "and last night I could hear voices whispering around me. I felt better when I went out but this massive dog in the woods scared the living daylights out of me. Guess I was still jumpy after all."

"What dog?"

"I don't know, I've never seen anything like it before. It was huge and shaggy, really black hair. It didn't seem to have an owner. It followed me for a while. Probably belonged to one of the tourists."

Robyn was so intent on picking up the last few crystals and thinking how this was the second time in two days that her attention had been drawn to them that she missed the worried look on Julianne's face.

They headed over to the pub at about seven to meet up with Jim and Fiona and have something to eat. Bryn came to join them with the dark haired man Robyn had seen busking.

"This is Holly," Bryn said.

Holly took Robyn's hand and kissed it. "Enchanted," he said, winking at her again. Julianne raised her eyebrows.

"Holly, you are incorrigible," she sighed.

"All part of my charm."

"You look pale," Jim said to Robyn. "Are you OK?"

"She's had some really horrible dreams," Julianne said, ignoring Robyn's warning glare. "Trying to find something, can't get to where she's going, that sort of thing."

Holly and Bryn both stared at her. "That sounds mighty unpleasant," Holly said.

Robyn could feel herself blushing under the scrutiny. "It's no big deal," she countered quickly. "Just leftover exam stress and..." She shrugged. "It'll pass."

"Dreams sometimes hold the key to more than just the obvious," Fiona commented. "Maybe there's something else you're looking for."

"Honestly, I'd rather forget them than interpret them right now." Robyn was becoming quite uncomfortable. "They scare me at night. I'd rather not think about them during the day if you don't mind." She chose to ignore the look that passed between Julianne and Fiona.

"Let us distract you with music then," Bryn said, lightening the atmosphere. "Come on Holly, we're on in ten minutes." As they left, he turned back and smiled, and Robyn knew somehow that smile was just for her.

The band was amazing. They played two forty minute sets and the whole place was on its feet. Robyn couldn't keep still. She danced and danced and somehow the music drained the tension right out of her.

"You guys are so fantastic," she said from the seat she had fallen into in post frenzy exhaustion.

"Glad you enjoyed it." Bryn dropped into the chair next to her.

"That was such a blast," Holly grinned.

"You do just keep getting better," Fiona added.

"Why, thank you," Holly said. "So nice to have our brilliance recognised."

They were all laughing when Holly looked up suddenly. "Sorry, guys, I've got to go." He stood up.

"Is everything OK?" That was Bryn.

Holly nodded. "Just need to catch up with someone. See you soon." He hurried out.

"Is he OK?" Robyn asked. "He looked a bit worried."

"I'm sure he's fine," Bryn assured her. "He'll let us know if there's a problem." He smiled, although Robyn thought she could detect a hint of concern in his face.

"Unfortunately, I don't know him well enough to ask him about it," she thought.

They sat talking until closing time then Bryn went to help load the music kit back into the van. Jim and Robyn went over to see if they could help, carrying an assortment of amplifiers, boxes and stands outside.

"Thanks," said Luke, the drummer. "Can we hire you as roadies?"

"Not likely," said Jim.

"That was so amazing," Robyn said again, as they gathered by the van.

"Glad you could make it," Bryn grinned.

"Yeah, come and see us again. And spread the word," Luke said, smiling broadly. "OK Bryn, see you back at yours."

"Great," Bryn said. "Well goodbye all. See you soon. Julianne, I'll let you know when I find out, OK?"

Julianne nodded.

"Bye," Robyn said. Bryn gave her that smile again, the one that warmed her all the way to her toes. Then he walked away down the road. A few minutes later the gorgeous black and silver bike she had seen a few days before drove past them, the rider waving as he went.

"Was that Bryn?" Robyn asked. Jim nodded. "That's such a fantastic bike."

"I'm sure if you ask him nicely he'll take you for a ride," Fiona said, nudging her pointedly. Robyn glared at her. "Oh, are you blushing?"

"Stop it, will you?" Robyn cuffed her gently. "Honestly!"

Fiona shrugged, laughing. "You're such a wind up merchant," Robyn continued. "And me with my heart broken and all." Although as she said it she realised that she didn't feel as crushed as she had done.

"So sorry." Fiona tried to put on a serious face. "But you know, they're not all frogs. He certainly isn't. He's definitely a knight. With a mean steed to prove it."

"Oh, Fiona, you're nuts." Robyn hugged her friend. "And I'm going home before you embarrass me anymore."

She said her goodbyes and headed back to the Dragon's Rest.

Chapter 5

THE weather was not good the following day. Thunder rumbled frequently in the distance and sharp showers dogged the holiday makers. It was great for the shop, and Robyn was kept busy all morning chatting to, advising and serving the customers. There were all sorts of people coming in and it always made her smile to hear the exclamations of the kids when they first saw the dragon. She only really noticed the dark haired woman because she had hovered uncertainly in the middle of the shop for several moments, looking on edge.

Robyn finished talking to the customer she was with and crossed over to speak to her. "Can I help you?"

The woman looked at her intensely. She had the deepest emerald green eyes that Robyn had ever seen. "I was hoping to see Holly," she said. "Or Julianne."

"Holly." Robyn was surprised. "I've never seen him in here. And Julianne won't be in 'til one. You could come back later or I can give her a message if you prefer." "I seem to have turned into J's messaging service," she couldn't help thinking.

The woman looked nervously round the shop. "I can't stay," she said. "It's too risky. I'll not hold out long enough." Robyn looked at her, mystified, noticing how pale she was.

"Are you ill," she asked, concerned. "Can I get you some water? Or call someone to help you?"

The woman smiled. "If only," she said. "You're very kind to offer but no. I need to get back... home." She beckoned Robyn over to a quiet corner and spoke under her breath. "Please tell Julianne or Holly that the breach has accelerated. We must hurry."

"The breach has accelerated, we must hurry," Robyn repeated, baffled.

"I'm sorry, I don't understand. What breach?"

The woman looked at her intently. "You will understand soon," she said. "Maybe more than you would wish. But that is up to them. Please pass the message on. It is vital that they know as soon as possible."

"Of course," Robyn said. The look of worry in the woman's eyes reminded her of what she had seen on the faces of Jim and Julianne recently. And, come to think of it, Bryn as he had watched Holly leave the night before. "Is Holly OK?"

The woman nodded. "Can I do anything for you?" Robyn was worried. "You look very pale."

She smiled. "No, thank you. Really. I just need to return home."

"Can I at least know your name?" Robyn asked. "So I can tell J who left the message."

The woman hesitated then smiled. "Oonagh is my name, Robyn. Maybe I'll see you again before this is done." She reached out and squeezed Robyn's shoulder and Robyn felt a tingle of electricity run through her. Before she had a chance to reply, or even to ask how she knew her name, the woman had gone.

Julianne became very flustered when Robyn told her about Oonagh's visit, and looked positively horrified when the message was relayed. "Has Holly been in?" she asked. "Or Bryn?" I must let Jim know and... I must text..."

"Whoa," Robyn said, standing up and putting her hand on her friend's shoulder. "What is going on, J? I've never seen you like this. And Jim isn't his usual carefree self either. Please, tell me, let me help."

Julianne was shaking her head. "I don't want to put you in that position," she said. Her eyes looked frantic.

"Please, J. This Oonagh said I would understand soon enough. Why won't you tell me?"

Julianne looked at her sharply. "Did she really say that?"

Robyn held up her hand. "Really. I promise."

Julianne hesitated. "OK look, I need to speak to Holly and Jim. Would you mind watching the shop for me this afternoon? I'll come back at closing and we'll talk then."

"Promise?"

"Promise." Julianne hesitated. "Robyn, don't think it's because I don't trust you, because it's not, it's just if I can keep you out of it, I'd rather."

"J, what...?" But Julianne was already heading out of the door. "OK then, see you later."

Julianne re-appeared as promised just as Robyn had finished locking up. Bryn was with her and they both looked serious.

"Hey guys," she said. "I was just going to have a bit of a tidy up."

"Don't worry about that now." Julianne's voice was quiet. "We need to talk to you about something important, but I think you should come and sit down."

"Is this about what's been going on? Can I help?"

"What do you know?" Bryn asked, seeming a little surprised that she knew anything at all.

"Nothing much. Only that there's some problem that's got J and Jim stressed out like I've never seen them. And that J's reticent to tell me anything or let me help because... I don't really know why, some risk she perceives, I s'pose."

"Yeah," Bryn said. "She wanted to try and protect you but unfortunately I think you're already involved."

"Bryn." Julianne's voice held a warning.

"Involved in what? What is going on? Are you part of this too?"

"Robyn, come and sit down and we'll tell you everything. Please." Julianne led them into the kitchen. "This is not going to be easy to explain."

Robyn sat down as requested and looked at them hard. They were both obviously uncomfortable, looking at each other for reassurance. "Do you want to start?" Julianne asked.

"If you want me to," Bryn replied.

Robyn was becoming increasingly frustrated. She drummed her fingers on the table. "Would one of you please just tell me?"

"OK, OK." Julianne took a deep breath. "This is going to sound so farfetched, but I can't make it any other way. You know the other day when we were sitting here in the twilight and I asked you if you thought there might be other planes of existence, other beings?" Robyn nodded, mystified. "Well I wasn't really asking rhetorically. I wanted to introduce the idea just in case it came to this."

"But we've talked about the spirit realm before. And the likelihood of other trans-dimensional planes that we're parallel with. It's one of Jim's pet theories, I don't have to tell you that."

"This is different. It's not a theory any more. They exist, Robyn. At least, we know that there is one other realm at least, linked to this one but kept separate by a protective shield."

"And there are other beings that live there, magical beings," Bryn added.

Robyn just stared at them.

"But there's an issue with the shield. It's damaged and now both worlds are in danger. That's what our problem is."

"The other side can't maintain it for much longer. And if we can't fix it…"

"You're kidding me, right. This is a joke?" Robyn tried to smile as she broke into what Bryn was saying, but the irritation was evident in her voice. However Julianne and Bryn still looked deadly serious. Their words came tumbling out faster now, as if desperate to convince her.

"I wish it was but unfortunately not," Julianne said.

"No," Bryn continued. "It really isn't. Holly's trying to help us. He comes from the other side, he can cross over between the worlds like some of them can. Like Oonagh."

"But more and more of them are getting through, some that shouldn't be able to, like the dog you saw yesterday."

"And we think you are involved somehow. Because of the timing and because of the dreams you've been having. We think they may hold an answer."

"Do you know what you sound like?" Robyn shook her head, unable to decide whether to laugh or shout at them. She remembered with a lurch the way Bryn had smiled at her the evening before. She hadn't thought he was the sort of person who would make fun of her like this.

"I know it sounds crazy but it's no joke." That came from Julianne.

"It's the truth." Bryn backed her up.

Robyn was beyond irritated now. "Guys, this isn't funny."

"Robyn, I'm not trying to tease you, honestly, you know I wouldn't…"

Robyn cut Julianne off mid-sentence. "Look, enough OK. I can take a wind up, but I don't like it when people try to make a fool of me. Please, just stop."

She got up and stalked out of the kitchen, back into the shop where she could usually find some calm. But not this evening. Because although she hated to admit it, what they had said had had a ring of truth to it, especially when she thought about her nightmares. She walked over to where the candles were, trying to slow her breathing, quell the feeling in her chest. She so wanted it to be anger but it felt more like panic.

"Robyn." They had followed her in, were standing by the counter, waiting for her reaction. She kept her back to them.

"Just leave me alone." It was a whisper that came out. A moment later there was a hand, gentle on her shoulder. She stiffened.

"I'm sorry Robyn." Bryn spoke softly. "I know it's a lot to take in, let alone accept. I felt the same when I first found out the truth. I didn't speak to Holly for a month because I thought he was laughing at me behind my back with the other kids, and he was my best friend. But he wasn't joking. The magic realm is real, and if I had a way of proving it to you right now I would. But I don't. I'm human and I can't use magic. Julianne and I can only tell you what we know and hope that you trust us enough to believe us."

Robyn turned round to them then and looked each of them in the eye for a long moment. She felt herself soften as they steadily held her gaze. Eventually she sighed. "I believe that you believe it. And since I know Julianne wouldn't lie to me, and you're her friend so by association you wouldn't lie either, I guess I have to believe it too. But it's going to take a while to get my head around it."

"We understand," Julianne said, taking her hand. "But unfortunately time is not on our side. We are closer to it now than we've ever been, but so are they. And we've had word that he is on the move."

"He who? What is *it*?" Robyn said. Bryn and Julianne exchanged a look.

"I'm not sure if you're ready for the whole thing right now," Julianne began, but the look on Bryn's face suddenly changed. She glanced at him, a question in her eyes.

"Incoming message," Bryn said. He looked at Robyn. "This may help to convince you that we haven't both gone mad."

He lifted his T shirt, baring his abdomen, and Robyn gasped in shock. Words were appearing, as if from nowhere, on his skin. She couldn't tear her eyes away as several sentences wrote themselves across Bryn's stomach.

"What the heck is that?"

"Holly. It's the quickest way to communicate if there's something urgent." He bent forward slightly, in order to read the words. "The breaches have widened. More will be through soon."

Julianne's face paled. "Is he...?"

"I think Holly would have said so," Bryn said. "We're OK for now, but probably not much longer. And the fact that he uses breaches, plural, isn't a good sign."

"What do we do?" Julianne asked. Robyn shook her head to clear it and spoke as decisively as she could.

"You come with me into the kitchen and you tell me everything, no matter how nuts it sounds. Don't worry, I'll deal with it."

She went ahead of them and put the kettle on, made tea mainly to keep her hands busy and try to stop them from shaking. They sat round the little table and Bryn began.

"I've known Holly since I was about nine. He was always around, used to join in with a group of us that played football and went beach combing and generally hung about making nuisances of ourselves. I never really questioned why he never went to school with us. I asked him once and he said he learned from his parents, so we all thought he was home taught. He always seemed a bit different, but he was such a daredevil and led us into such wild escapades that no one really cared. When we went on to senior school, the others drifted away but he and I still got on. That was when I started playing the guitar and realised he could play the pipe.

I only found out that he was fey the summer that I took my GCSEs. The first breach had occurred and the faerie elders wanted to pull in some more support from this side to help heal it. So he told me that he came from the magical realm and that he wasn't human but faerie that could use magic. And that there was a problem."

Bryn paused. "I didn't take it very well. I thought he was trying to get back in with the others by making an idiot of me. Even when he showed me his ears. I didn't speak to him for weeks."

"His ears?" Robyn interjected.

"Yeah. Long and pointed. It's not just the rock god image that makes him keep his hair long although he does keep them glamoured a lot of the time. Anyway, eventually he got through to me by sending me a message. Just like you saw earlier. Some spell cast by a faerie elder allowed him to do it. It totally freaked me out, but I couldn't deny the truth of what he'd told me. So of course, if he was real, the problem was real too, and I couldn't not help a friend, could I?"

"So what was the problem?"

"You need a potted version of faerie history. The fey were one of the earliest peoples, and originally they lived side by side with humans. But gradually humans became dominant – they were aggressive and so interested in science and technological development that they began to lose their connection with magic and the natural balance of the earth. The further they pushed, the more the fey withdrew underground. Hence the myths and legends worldwide of fairy mounds and magical doors and such like. Some really are myths, some are true but most are somewhere in between. The more the humans spread and changed the land and built and polluted, the more the magical realm retreated. Eventually, the human way became intolerable for most of them and the elders of light and dark magic agreed that it would be better to withdraw completely. They created a protective shield to separate the faerie and human realms, impenetrable to most on both sides. It's been that way ever since, a secret guarded by trusted entities on both sides. In fact, so successfully that we're as much a myth to most of them as they are to us."

"Why do I feel a 'but' coming on?" Robyn queried.

Julianne took up the story. "Because just as science and technology have advanced on this side, so magic has advanced over there. And just before Jim and I moved here, what, seventeen, eighteen years ago, a fragment of the shield had somehow become separated from the rest of it and had been lost on this side. No one thought it was very important, the Elders repaired the damage and things went on as normal."

"But it seemed that the damage had been greater than they thought." Bryn continued. "And of course on that side, same as here, not everyone has good intentions. There were dark practitioners who concentrated on the area that the fragment had been lost from and gradually developed a web of tiny cracks across the shield."

"The cracks were so minute that they went unnoticed." That was Julianne. "But they had weakened the integrity of the shield and breaches began to open up. Miniscule at first and spread far apart. It was about four years ago when the elders realised the extent of the problem. That was when Jim and I found out about the other world as well."

"Did you know Holly too?"

"Only by sight." Julianne hesitated. "It was Fiona that told us."

"Fiona!" Robyn was astounded. Fiona was one of the most matter of fact people she knew. The thought of her being in contact with otherworldly beings was incongruous to say the least. "Oh my goodness. Is she..."

"She's human, if that's what you're going to ask. But she's a witch with some psychic ability and so she's one of the people on this side who protect the shield. I think she realised that Jim and I had such a deep interest in things out there," Julianne waved her hand vaguely in the air, "that maybe she could draw us in to help."

Robyn got up from the table.

"We're not quite finished yet," Bryn said.

"I guessed that," Robyn concurred, opening the fridge. She returned to the table with three bottles of beer and an opener. "Sorry, but I need something a little stronger than tea."

"So," Julianne went on, "in the last four years the cracks have continued to deepen and spread, and the breaches have become larger and more numerous. Repair held them at bay initially, but the amount of energy and magic required to hold the shield together is becoming unsustainable. And the bigger the breaches are, the more crossover becomes possible."

"But crossover has always been possible, hasn't it?" Robyn asked, looking at Bryn. "Otherwise you never would have met Holly."

"True," said Bryn. "There have always been some on both sides who could travel between. Usually protectors, but some chance crossings and others for malevolent purposes. When it was limited, it was manageable for both sides. Here, bizarre events would be dismissed as the ravings of nutters with wild imaginations. There, non magical beings were looked on with derision or ignored as faulted. But it's becoming more and more difficult to control, and he is gathering his forces all the time, ready for when the shield breaks down entirely."

"Who is 'he'?"

"A dark practitioner. His name is Maric. He used to be high ranking in the Seelie court, but his loyalties lie only with himself. He was banished and the Unseelie court refused him refuge. So he remained solitary and has been gaining power for over two hundred years. Recently he formed his own court and has been gathering forces, wanting to…"

"Back up a bit," said Robyn. "What's Seelie?"

"The Seelie and Unseelie courts are generally regarded as the good fey and the bad fey, but it's more complex than that," Julianne explained. "There's more than one of each, I s'pose you could regard them as the government of their individual territories, and although each will be one or the other, Seelie or Unseelie, that doesn't make them intrinsically bad or good. It just makes them, umm, how can I put it?"

"Culturally different," Bryn finished. "The Seelie court is associated with light and the Unseelie with dark, just like the English are associated with, er... roast beef and the French with frog's legs."

Robyn couldn't contain herself. She let out a peal of hysterical laughter. The others stared at her in surprise as she shook helplessly.

"I'm sorry," she finally managed to stutter. "First you were talking about breaches and threats and presumably the end of the world as we know it and then, frog's legs!" It set her off again, and this time Julianne joined in.

"Well," said Bryn, his lips twitching. "It's a darn hard thing to find a metaphor for fairyland."

When they had all recovered their composure, Julianne took up the story again.

"So he has been weakening the shield and growing in strength, biding his time until the shield is down enough for them all to come through. There are more and more of his soldiers scouting around but they haven't been able to locate it any more than we have. I think he will try himself soon. And if he gets to it before we do..."

Silence fell, as bleak as the laughter had been joyous moments before.

"What is it that you're all looking for?" Robyn ventured finally.

"The lost piece of the shield," Bryn answered. "It's the only thing that will fully restore its integrity. No one knows exactly where it was lost, but since the biggest breach seems to be developing here it makes sense that it's somewhere around."

"But it could've been lost in the sea. It could be anywhere," Robyn cried.

"I know. But all the indications, the investigations and the scrying seem to indicate that it's nearby. In fact, in or near the village," Julianne said.

"What does it look like?"

"That's the problem," Bryn sighed. "Nobody knows. The general assumption is that it will look like a piece of crystal or glass but honestly," he sighed again, "it could be anything."

"But," Julianne chimed in, "the good news is you're here."

"What difference do I make?"

Bryn looked hard at Julianne, who nodded. "She needs to know."

"There is a prophecy," Bryn began carefully. "Holly told me about it.

That a girl would appear at the time of greatest need and restore what was lost to its place of rest." He was about to go on when Robyn held up her hand.

"Whoa there," she said. "You can't seriously think that's me. That's crazy."

"Actually, not really," Julianne countered. "You started coming here on holiday the year the first breach happened. You've been here each year since, and been drawn in here more every time. And this year, when things are really getting desperate, you came down earlier than planned. Add those coincidences to the dreams you told us about and really it's not so crazy after all."

More silence. Robyn drained the last of her beer.

"Right then," she said brightly. "Let me see if I've got this straight. You think that I, an ordinary girl from urbansville, am actually the... person... that is prophesied to save the world, no, two worlds, by finding an unknown object and putting it back in an unknown location before all the forces of hell are let loose and everything is lost?"

There was a heavy pause.

"That about sums it up," said Bryn.

"Well," said Robyn. Panic was rising. "What else do I need to know?"

It was late when Julianne and Bryn left. Julianne hugged her hard. "I'm so sorry," she kept saying.

Bryn touched her shoulder and passed her a piece of paper. "My mobile," he told her. "Any questions, any problems, any time, OK?"

"Thanks," she said quietly. She must have still looked overwhelmed because he bent down so he could look in her eyes.

"Anything, any time. Even if you think it's daft or it can wait."

She nodded. She couldn't find her voice.

"Get some sleep. I'm sorry we had to land all this on you."

She shrugged. "And I always used to like surprises," she joked lamely.

"It'll be OK," Bryn said reassuringly. "Try not to worry." He smiled at her and despite her concern she felt her heart flutter. "Goodnight."

"Night."

Chapter 6

ROBYN found it difficult to sleep at all. Her head was spinning with all the information she had been given. Not just about the shield and the fey and dark practitioners and Holly and Fiona, but about the charms and magical protection that had been put on the shop, and the fact that they all seemed to think that she was going to be able to find this thing that no one else on either side could track down. The sleep she did get was dream torn and disturbed but this time she had no memory of any nightmares, just a deep feeling of unease.

She got up early, not wanting to drift in and out of sleep any longer, and went down to do the tidying in the shop that she had been distracted from the night before. It was a calming place to be and she took her time straightening and rearranging, breathing in the incense that still hung in the air. She opened the windows and coaxed out two butterflies that had appeared on the panes.

"You won't be happy in here," she told them. "Go on, out into the fresh air. And you, my friend," she said to the spider that was climbing over one of Fiona's fairy statuettes, "you're either mighty determined or you have a twin living in my kitchen. Come on, out or you'll get squished by some tourist and we don't want that, do we?" She put the spider up by the opening. By the time Julianne and Jim arrived at half past eight she had lit the candles and was just about to open up. Jim gave her a hug.

"How are you? After hearing about everything?"

"Bemused and befuddled," Robyn said. "I can't even think of any questions to ask. I nearly get one and then my brain turns to cotton wool and it disappears."

"Don't worry, it's a lot to take in. It'll get easier."

Robyn stayed in the shop that morning, even though Julianne had said she could have the day off. She knew the shop, knew how it ran and it felt like the safest place to be, given that her world had just turned upside down. There was a constant flow of customers in so she didn't really have a chance to talk any more about it to the others, but she was glad of the distraction. It all seemed so normal, she could almost pretend that Bryn and Julianne had been having her on. Almost. But there was no way she could think of that Bryn could have made that writing appear on his skin. There was no denying how serious they had both been. And her dreams had always been vivid enough that even when she couldn't really remember them they had left her feeling that something wasn't right.

And now, thinking back over the past few months, the unprecedented extremes of weather, the odd events that she had read about in the newspapers, the sudden increase in violent crime and civil unrest that seemed to be on every news programme she had seen for the last goodness only knew how long, she couldn't help but realise that it was all connected. If the balance was off and negative forces wanted to take over, it would make it so much easier for them if the human world was in disarray beforehand.

Robyn shivered despite the heat and the closeness of the day. It was hard not to feel overwhelmed when she thought about everything. And yet she could still chat and laugh with the visitors to the shop as if there was nothing untoward going on at all. She felt as though she was observing herself from the sidelines, trying to grasp at something that just kept running away from her, like sand through her fingers.

Fiona appeared at midday. Robyn, feeling oddly shy and more than a little confused, stayed over by the CDs and pretended she hadn't seen. She half-heartedly started to tidy them back into alphabetical order, aware that Fiona was talking to Julianne and Jim and that they were all looking at her. It was on days like this, Robyn realised, that she was relieved she had her own style. The heavy eyeliner was quite handy to hide behind, and if you had that Goth type look, no one expected you to be smiling all the time.

Eventually Fiona came over to her. "Hi," she said. "How are you?"

"Fine," Robyn said instinctively. She paused. "Actually, no. Not fine. Confused. At a loss. Feeling a little..." she had to think hard to find the right word, "betrayed actually, though I'm sure it seems unreasonable given the circumstances." She realised there was anger in her voice.

"I can understand that," Fiona said gently. "If we had known we would have told you sooner, but you know hindsight is a great thing after the fact. And we didn't want to involve anyone unnecessarily because of the risks."

Robyn's shoulders slumped. "I know that, and I probably would have done the same in your shoes. But my head is still spinning and I feel like I should somehow have known. And that because I didn't I've let everyone down, including myself."

"Robyn, that's daft. How could you have known? It's only circumstance that any of us found out. It could easily have been other people instead."

Robyn shrugged. It just all felt like too much.

"Come on," said Fiona. "Julianne says I can borrow you this afternoon. There are some things I want to show you but first you need something to eat. You're paler than a pale thing and I'm not talking about your make up."

They walked back to Fiona's cottage where Fiona fed her soup and bread and chocolate muffins. Then they went to sit outside under the shade of the big beech tree, watching the dragonflies flit over the pond.

"I understand how much of a shock this must have been," Fiona began carefully. "I remember when I had to tell Julianne, how dazed she felt for ages. And you don't even have the luxury of time to get used to it because the threat is imminent. I'm sorry for that. But there is always a reason for everything, the whys and the wherefores of being in a certain place at a certain time or turning right instead of left or whatever, and we are sure that the reason you're here now, that you came down early was to help us find this missing piece."

The scientific logical part of Robyn's brain was trying to make her shout "Reason for everything? Destiny and all that? Crap." But she managed to bite it back because the other bit of her, the part that wanted to believe in the magical, the unseen, the unknown, was craving more knowledge.

"So what happens now? What am I supposed to do? I feel like I should have all the answers if I'm really this person that's supposed to restore the shield, and I don't know anything. And how can I fix something that I can't even see?"

"You'll be in the right place at the right time and you'll know what to do. I'm sorry, I know it sounds nebulous but it's the truth. Sometimes you don't have to know something consciously to hold the knowledge. It just is in you. And even though you can't see the shield, you'll be able to see a break in it."

"Have you ever been over there?" Robyn wanted to know.

Fiona nodded. "A few times, when I was learning. Oonagh took me across. She was my mentor."

"The lady I met the other day?"

"Yes. She taught me to use magic so that I could help protect the shield and the secret from this side. I was able to help keep the balance until the last couple of years. But there's been such an increase in the number of incursions from the other side it's become impossible. And it's happening everywhere even though the most active place is here at the site of the original damage."

Robyn mentioned what had occurred to her earlier about crime and unrest and odd weather. Fiona sighed. "It's all related in some way. Magic tends to magnify things that would happen naturally and make them more extreme. But that can be good as well as bad. I'm aware that all you've really heard is the negative scary stuff, but there's some amazing and good stuff too. Like Holly and his piping and the way it hangs around in your head for hours making you smile. Healing balms and potions. The way you can sometimes see a reflection of the magical and it lifts your heart, even though you don't know why."

"Reflection?"

"Yeah, unexpected little things that you may not even be aware of, like rainbows, the colours on the surface of a bubble, that amazing light you sometimes get before a storm. The things that give you the sensation of something extraordinary that's really hard to put into words but that stays with you for no apparent reason."

"Oh." Oddly, Robyn knew exactly what Fiona meant. She thought of the hydrangeas in the twilight.

"I want to show you something that is pure good magic," Fiona went on. "She helps me, strengthens my ability because she's from the other side." She held her hand out in front of her. "Silver. Come and meet Robyn."

There was a fluttering and a glint of shimmering turquoise, and one of the dragonflies that constantly flew over Fiona's pond alighted on her finger. Robyn gasped. She had never seen one up so close, let alone settling on a human. The creature turned her dazzling bejewelled eyes to Robyn.

"Silver chose to become my familiar one of the times I went across with Oonagh. She's helped me so much, she connects me with the other realm and makes such a difference."

"She's beautiful."

"Silver, what can you tell Robyn?"

Silver delicately left Fiona's finger and landed softly on Robyn's shoulder. Robyn hardly dared to breathe. She became aware of a tingle, like electricity, under the dragonfly's tiny feet – it followed her footsteps as she walked gently down Robyn's arm to her hand. Then she rose into the air and wheeled back to the pond.

"Did you feel anything?" Fiona wanted to know.

"It was a bit like an electrical tingling. The same as I felt when Oonagh touched my arm. What is it?"

"It's the way the body processes magical energy. You'll get used to it. It's useful for picking up who's what."

"I didn't get it from Holly though."

"Holly spends a lot of his time over here. He doesn't… didn't use magic a great deal until recently, when he's had no choice and he's learned to contain his magical energy. Also he doesn't have a huge amount of power. Powerful beings like Oonagh or the other elders come across only rarely and can't always reign it in enough. They also find this realm drains them quite rapidly. That was why we needed to tell you yesterday what was going on. Oonagh would only have come in an emergency."

"Is that why she looked so pale and tired?"

"Probably. Robyn, I need to tell you some things about protecting yourself from the fey that have negative intentions towards you. Much as I wish you weren't at risk, you are, and you need to know what to do should you come up against them." Fiona got up. "Come inside with me and I'll show you."

It was gone seven when Robyn got back to the shop, and Holly and Bryn were waiting for her in the kitchen.

"Hey," said Bryn. "The Js went home about half an hour ago. We said we'd hang on for you."

"Wanted to make sure you were OK." Holly added. He wore his customary grin but there was concern clouding his eyes. And now

Robyn came to think of it, they were green eyes, not as startling as Oonagh's but still green.

"Actually, I am OK, thanks," she smiled, and was surprised and touched to see the relief on both their faces. She didn't think it was just because they needed her as their prophecy girl.

"Do you feel like coming out with us for the evening then? There's a band playing over in Thornwood that we were going to go and see," Bryn asked. "You had a horrible evening yesterday because of what I told you, I'd kind of like to make it up to you if I can."

"It's not your fault Bryn. You don't have to."

He smiled at her then. "But I'd like to."

Holly nudged him. "We'd like to."

"In that case, I'd love to. Give me ten minutes to change?"

Holly took Bryn's bike over to Thornwood. Bryn had borrowed his father's car to drive Robyn and himself there. "Holly has trouble in cars. Being stuck in an iron box is a faerie's nightmare," he said.

"Why does iron affect them so much?"

"I don't know," Bryn confessed. "Holly might be able to tell you."

The pub was already busy when they got there and it wasn't long until the band came on. It was impossible to stay still to the lively folk music they played. Holly obviously liked to dance and was leaping about like a mad thing, whirling Robyn around until she was dizzy with laughter. Bryn stomped in a more sedate manner, but Robyn was very aware of him. She caught his eye more than once, enjoying the smile he gave her, the butterflies it loosed in her chest.

At the end of the first set they flung themselves into seats to get their breath back.

"They're good," said Robyn. "But not as good as you guys."

Holly flamboyantly kissed her hand. "You're too kind." Bryn just smiled.

"No, really, I mean it."

"How'd we get so lucky?" Holly said to Bryn. "Beautiful and brilliant."

Bryn was still smiling. Robyn shook her head. "You are a dreadful flirt, Holly," she scolded him. "Stop it."

Holly put his hand on his heart. "I'm crushed."

"Yeah, right. Of course you are," she laughed. "So, who's the Tolkein fan then?"

Bryn and Holly exchanged glances.

"What makes you think either of us are?" Bryn said.

"I doubt your band would have its name if someone wasn't. Underhill. Come on. But then I suppose it might be one of the others."

"I'm impressed," Bryn said. "OK, I confess, it's me. Although Holly has a bit of a soft spot for him too."

"True," Holly grinned. "He's entertaining to read but he took a lot of liberties with the facts."

Robyn looked at him sharply. "Huh?"

"Yeah. Some of it is based on the truth. Tolkein had friends from our side. It's probably what sparked his ideas in the first place. But most of it is fiction."

Robyn slumped back in her chair. "What, so all those characters, creatures, they all..."

Holly laughed. "No. That's what I mean. Most of them are completely imaginary. But some of the wars and the distrust; it wasn't so much between races as between the faerie courts. Like many of your wars are between countries."

"I always thought "The Lord Of The Rings" was a metaphor for World War 1."

"It is but not that alone. Our realm has had some long wars and huge battles just like here. It would seem that every creature in existence has a survival streak, and most a territorial streak too. Much as we may wish for peaceful coexistence, there are some who'll never be satisfied with anything less than complete domination." He sighed. "Not just over their own region, but the whole realm. And others. But we're not thinking about that tonight. Tonight is for music and revelry and fun. And talking of music, I think the band are about to start up again. Come on." And grabbing Robyn's hand, he whirled her back into the crowd.

After the second set had finished they sat outside with a last drink to cool off. The clouds had gone and the sky was bright with stars. Robyn looked up and sighed. "That's one of the things I love down here. How clear the stars are. There's too much light where I live."

"Most people don't even give it a thought," Holly said.

"She's not most people, is she?" Bryn winked at her. "Or hadn't you noticed?"

Holly gave her an exaggerated stare then clapped his hand to his head and theatrically pretended to fall off the seat. "Of course. How could I have been so stupid?"

"Not stupid, but just a little ridiculous maybe," Robyn giggled, blushing. Holly scrambled back up onto the bench.

"Just a little bit," Bryn agreed.

"Never a truer word was said," Holly laughed. "But where would we be without the ridiculous and the unbelievable, pray tell?"

"Still in blissful ignorance," Robyn said, and couldn't help laughing when they both looked at her anxiously. "Don't stress, I'm not going to freak out on you. Well, not tonight anyway."

"You almost had me worried there," Holly said thankfully.

"Almost?" Robyn queried, raising her eyebrows. "Oh well, I'll have to try harder next time."

"And I will surely be lost," Holly replied. "If not in worry, in your eyes of deepest... brown? Grey?" He stared into her face. "Heck, I can't see."

"Grey," Robyn and Bryn said together.

"Grey, right." Holly smirked at Bryn. "Well, obviously your powers of observation are better than mine, partner."

"Not to mention my memory and my ability to run a class with some semblance of order." Bryn's tone was stern but his eyes were laughing.

"So true," Holly capitulated. "But again, where would we be without the ridiculous and the unbelievable?" He stood up and gave them a deep bow. "And with that thought to ponder, I bid you goodnight. It's been a delectable evening. I'll leave the bike at yours, Bryn. See you anon." He sauntered off towards the car park.

"Is he ever serious?" Robyn asked. "What was that all about?"

"Not serious often, it has to be said," Bryn replied. "But yes, when he needs to be. The day he came to "help" me with my class it was more like a riot."

"What class?"

"Oh, I run a basic rock guitar class for the local kids every Monday morning. Just for an hour and a half. I did it last summer as well. I get them to pick some songs at the beginning of the summer, then I can work out the parts and adjust for different levels of ability. They're a really good bunch and they seem to enjoy it."

"So what happened when Holly turned up?"

"Well, he plays a bit of guitar too, so I told him to just bring that. And his pipe if he wanted. But he "forgot" what I'd told him and turned up with his guitar, his pipe and his bodhran, plus some other percussion stuff. And a bass drum with a double pedal, and a hi-hat. So naturally all the kids wanted a go on everything, and it was all pretty chaotic. Just to confuse matters even more, he decided to try and teach them a folk melody over the top of the rock song we were working on. And then he pulled a Jethro Tull on me, started leaping around the hall with his pipe like a lunatic, so all the kids who weren't attached to the bass drum or the hi-hat or an amp were leaping around after him. It was like watching the Pied Piper of Hamelin."

"What did you do?"

"Well, after trying and failing miserably to restore some order to the proceedings, I did the only thing I could." Bryn laughed at the memory. "Put down my electric guitar, picked up my acoustic and joined in."

"Sounds hysterical," Robyn said.

"I nearly was by the end, but it was fun. It always is. Hey, maybe you should pop in and say hi."

"But I don't play anything."

"Doesn't matter. And at the risk of using you shamelessly, you'd be great for my image. The kick ass, Goth rock thing you've got going is very cool. Since they've had the Holly experience, they think I'm a boring old fogey."

"Yeah," said Robyn. "With the tattoos and the hair and the guitar and the bike, I'm sure that's exactly what they think." She tried to keep a straight face but he gave her such a quizzical look, she couldn't. Moments later he was laughing too.

"OK, OK, point taken. But really, it'd be really nice if you did drop in. Ten 'til eleven thirty at the Village Hall."

"I'll try. It depends if I'm on my own in the shop, but if I'm not I'll try and get there. And I promise I won't lead them into any bad ways."

"I appreciate that. But it might be fun to watch you try."

"Don't tempt me."

Bryn looked at his watch. "They'll be kicking us out soon. Perhaps we'd better go."

"Probably. I really enjoyed this evening," Robyn told him. "Thanks for letting me crash your lads night."

"It wasn't really, but you can crash my evening any time."

Robyn looked down at her hands, feeling her colour rise again.

"I enjoy your company," Bryn went on. "I like people who are individual, who don't feel they have to follow the clones." He looked approvingly at her attire, the black top and purple skirt that she had bought that day with Cara. "People who are open to thinking outside the norm."

"I enjoy your company too," Robyn said. His directness was a little disconcerting but she made herself look at him despite the shyness she felt and it melted away in the warmth of his eyes.

They sat for a while talking in the car outside the shop when he dropped her off, and he insisted on walking her to the door and seeing her inside. "See you soon," he said as he left.

Chapter 7

THE following morning, after she had helped Jim unpack some new stock and put it out, she asked if he minded her having a couple of hours off.

"I know I wasn't much help yesterday," she said, "but I just need to go walking for a bit and try and get everything straight in my head."

"Of course you can," Jim said. "Julianne's coming in later anyway and I don't have to leave 'til two. Take as long as you need."

Robyn let herself out of the back door and followed the footpath away from the street towards the fields. Although she loved the woods the thought of the huge dog put her off, so she headed out toward the sea and the path along the Overcliff. Walking along with the rush of the breeze, the sultry heat of the clouded sun on her back and the waves singing in her ears, she allowed her mind to wander, trying to make sense of the last few days. She made it up to the highest point on that section of coastline and sat for a while, trying to think of nothing at all. It was impossible. Holly and Fiona and Bryn all kept appearing in her head, Bryn particularly and for not just magic related reasons.

"For goodness sake," she scolded herself when she found she was thinking about how well defined his arms were especially when he was playing the guitar. "Get a grip." She realised that it was making her feel guilty, this attraction to Bryn, as if somehow she was being disloyal to Anthony, or at least to how she had felt about him. But her feelings had changed. In fact everything had changed. She got up and dusted herself down. "Time to go back to work."

Heading back along the path Robyn was, as always, lost in the view. The stepped cliffs and ragged rocks gave the impression of something wild and desperate clinging on to the land by its fingernails, while the relentless beat of the sea tried to prise it away and drag it down. The raw beauty never failed to steal her breath. She stopped again for a moment, shielding her eyes from the bright light and staring out across the impossible blue green of the water.

There was a sharp stinging sensation on her left calf. Instinctively she reached down and rubbed it, thinking that she had been stung. Several seconds later, there was another on her hip, more of a blow this time, and then again on her shoulder. Robyn began to walk but the strikes continued and she noticed that small pebbles were falling all around her. There was a chittering in the scrubby grass and gorse either side of the path, high pitched spiteful laughter, leaves rustling and twigs snapping despite the stillness of the air. Robyn broke into a jog then a run as the stones became a hailstorm. She could just make out creatures in the grass, small twiggy limbed figures with long noses and angry eyes. There seemed to be a lot of them. And then the first one leapt onto her back, its gnarly fingers yanking at her hair.

"Get off me," she shrieked, grabbing frantically behind her and flinging it away by its spindly arm. Another one had attached itself to her leg. Stones were still raining down on her, dust rising around her as she ran. Panic was nearly choking her now as she felt more of them grabbing at her, leaping in front of her, trying to trip her and bring her down. She stumbled, twisting her ankle but managing to keep her footing, slowing under the onslaught of pinching and scratching and stones. Just as she felt that she couldn't go on, she heard Fiona's voice, a memory in her head. "There are charms that will protect you from the fey, should you need it. Salt's one, iron's another, they're the strongest. But red thread, bells and chimes, even turning your clothes inside out will work."

Robyn grabbed the bottom of her T shirt and wrenched it over her head, dislodging several of the little demons and sending them flying. Slowing momentarily, she flung it back on inside out, immediately relieved to find that the rest of them fell away. The storm of pebbles continued, however, and she accelerated back up to a run despite the pain in her ankle, not slowing until she reached the garden at the back of the shop. She fumbled desperately for her key, struggling to get it into the lock with her shaking hands, and flung herself through the kitchen door, collapsing onto one of the chairs as her knees gave way.

Jim was standing by the counter waiting for the kettle to boil.

"Crivens, girl, what on earth's happened?"

Robyn lent forward with her hands on her knees, trying to catch her breath. "Attacked," she managed to gasp. "Horrid little..."

Jim hurried over to her. "Are you hurt? Have they injured you? What were they?"

Still breathless, Robyn managed to confirm that she was OK. She could feel Jim gently removing twigs and other bits of detritus from her hair.

"Thanks," she said finally as her breathing settled. She looked up at him. His face was lined with concern.

"There's blood on you," he said, his tone worried. "You are hurt."

Robyn touched her face instinctively, becoming aware of several small cuts. "It probably looks worse than it is," she reassured him. "They were throwing stones and goodness only knows what else when they jumped me."

"Do you know what they were?"

"No. Small, skinny, twiggy looking things. There were loads of them, or at least it felt like there were."

Jim sat down opposite her. "Gremlins probably," he said. "Maybe redcaps. Some type of pack goblin, for sure. You did well to escape. They're like the fey equivalent of velociraptors, nasty vicious hunters who don't give up easily. How did you get away?"

Robyn indicated her T shirt, still inside out. "It was the only thing I could think of."

"Clever girl," Jim said. "Cool headed thinking in an extreme situation. It probably saved your life."

Robyn shivered. "Sorry," Jim apologised. "Probably not what you wanted to hear. But true, nonetheless." He stood up." I'm going to make you some tea, and then take over in the shop, let Julianne look at those cuts." Robyn was about to protest but he stopped her. "Just sit and rest."

Robyn sipped the hot sweet tea gratefully as Julianne came rushing in from the shop. "Oh sweetie," she said, horrified. "What have they done to you?"

Julianne bustled about with hot water and a cloth, and gently cleaned Robyn's cuts and grazes. Then she applied a balm. "It's something Fiona makes," she explained. "Eases the soreness and enhances healing. Now, do you feel up to telling me what happened? Jim's given me the gist of it but still."

Robyn explained where she'd been and why. "I just needed to try and make sense of everything," she said. "I was coming back along the path on the Overcliff, just looking out to sea when the stones started flying. Then they jumped me, it felt like they were all over me. So I turned my T shirt inside out and ran."

Julianne shook her head. "I so wish you didn't have to be involved in this. The last thing we want is for you to be in danger or injured."

"I know," said Robyn. "But it's OK. I am involved, for better or worse. It's fine. And I couldn't bear to think that nasty little things like that are running around hurting people. Let alone some of the other things that might come through if we, I, don't find this thing. So I'm in, one hundred percent, cuts and gremlins and all. If that's what they were."

"Probably," Julianne said. "Jim's pretty sure they were but he's just checking the books to make sure."

"So those books on fairy lore and myths and strange creatures, they're not just fairy tales and legends then?"

"Some of them." Julianne was grinning now. "But some of them are reference books."

"I had to ask, didn't I?" Robyn straightened up in her seat. "I feel much better now. I'll go and get changed and come down so Jim can get away. I'm sorry if I've made him late."

"Don't be ridiculous, you'll do no such thing. He can do his thing tomorrow, he's more than happy to stay. You need to go upstairs and have a nice shower and then take it easy. Rest this afternoon, let the ointment work. And when we close up I'll ask Fiona to come and reinforce the protection on the building so you'll be safe."

Robyn felt relief wash over her, tinged with guilt. "Are you sure?" she said. "I don't want to take advantage or ..."

"Let us down?" Julianne finished. Robyn nodded. "Sweetheart, you couldn't do that if you tried. Now go and get cleaned up and then just relax. Sleep if you can. We'll see you later."

Robyn rose and limped toward the door.

"Hey, what have I missed?" Julianne asked, following her.

"Oh nothing. I just turned my ankle when I was running. Never was much of an athlete, and dodgy ankles are part of the reason why. It'll be fine in a day or so."

"Take this." Julianne handed her the jar of balm. "Put some on after your shower. It'll help."

"Thanks, J."

After the shower had washed away the dust and some of the tension, Robyn settled down on the sofa with a book and tried to read, thinking that it would distract her. But she found that she couldn't concentrate, her mind close to overload with the inescapable evidence that reality was not the way she had accepted it was at all. So much had happened and even though she knew that the strange new world in which she found herself, and the entities she had encountered, both good and bad, were all real, part of her mind still fought against it. All the new information came rushing over her again, the impossible become the truth. It completely overwhelmed her. Exhausted, her brain gave itself an escape and dropped her into sleep, deep and for once, dreamless.

She came to several hours later, curled up on the sofa, her book open on the floor where it had fallen. It was still bright outside the window but the amber hue of the sunlight told her that it was late, definitely after closing time. She got up slowly, muscles feeling worse for wear after her enforced sprint, and went down to the kitchen, where she was sure she could hear voices.

Fiona, Jim and Julianne were sitting round the table, talking quietly.

"There you are," said Fiona, jumping up to hug her. "You've had a time and a half of it, haven't you?"

"You could say that," Robyn agreed. She sniffed appreciatively. "Something smells good."

"I took the liberty of making us something to eat," Jim said. "Here, sit down and I'll dish up. It's all ready."

While they ate the discussion centred on the increasing incursions of the more malevolent fey, such as the ones that had attacked her.

"I think Maric is aware of a change," Fiona mused. "The shield is weakening which makes it easier for him to send them over, and he probably knows that we are so much closer to finding the missing piece. He'll want to keep us distracted while he increases his efforts to get to it first."

"We're all going to have to be really careful," Jim said.

"And hope I can find it soon," Robyn added glumly. "I just wish we knew what to look for."

Julianne gazed at her sympathetically. "Try not to worry my lovely, something will come to you from one avenue or another."

Robyn sighed. "I so hope you're right."

Robyn was in the shop the whole of the following day. It was busy at times but in between she had time to think about the shield and the missing fragment and wonder how on earth she was supposed to find it. Even though the village, including its immediate surroundings, was not huge it still added up to a large area for the purposes of a search. And she didn't even know what she was looking for.

"I need help," she thought.

The next morning, Monday, Jim decided she needed a break. "Go and have fun for a couple of hours," he said.

Robyn wandered around for a bit and considered dropping in to see Fiona. Then something struck her, making her heart jump. Bryn's class was on. She stopped, wondering if she had the nerve. But she had questions about the fragment for him too, so she steeled herself and made for the village hall. It was half past ten when she got there and she could clearly hear the music coming from inside. She hesitated for a long moment and had strong words with herself.

"He invited you," she thought. "He wouldn't have if he hadn't meant it, he didn't have to say anything at all. And anyway there's a question you need to ask. You're not just turning up to... to..."

She couldn't bring herself to finish the sentence. She really liked Bryn, but the recent events with Anthony had made her cautious about her feelings and her judgement. However she did need to speak to him so, taking a deep breath, she pushed the door open quietly and slipped inside.

Bryn was over to her left, facing away from the door. Ranged around him were ten or eleven kids between the ages of about eight and twelve. They were watching him intently, playing chords as an echo to his while he kept the beat by tapping his foot. Robyn stood and watched, mesmerised by the look of concentration on all their faces.

"That's great guys," he said enthusiastically when they reached the end. "Now we're going to learn..."

"Er, Bryn," one of the boys said.

"Yes, Tom."

Tom pointed over at Robyn and all of a sudden she was the focus of a dozen pairs of eyes. She suddenly wished she'd never thought of this, that she could vanish without a trace, but Bryn had put down his guitar and was coming over to her, looking really pleased to see her. He took her hand and led her back across the hall.

"Guys, I'd like you to meet a friend of mine. This is Robyn."

Robyn put her hand up. "Hi," she managed to say. "You all sounded awesome."

Several of them smiled at that.

"We've been practising hard," said a little red haired girl to her right.

"You have, Mallory, and it obviously shows," Bryn said.

"Are you going to play like Holly did?" That came from the boy who was standing next to Tom.

"No," Robyn said. "I'm not talented like Holly and Bryn and you lot. I can't play an instrument. I just came to listen."

"Bryn could teach you," Mallory piped up.

"Yeah, he's a really good teacher," another little girl agreed.

"Well thank you, Vicki," Bryn said. Robyn was shaking her head but the boy next to Tom stepped forward.

"I'm Jared. You can borrow my guitar if you want."

"That's really kind of you, but I'd only hold you up," she said, to which there was an outcry. She looked desperately at Bryn for rescue but he was just smiling.

"Thanks Jared but it's OK. She can borrow mine." Bryn picked up his acoustic and slipped it over her head, adjusting the strap to fit her. "The people have spoken," he whispered softly in her ear, then "OK, now let's show Robyn how to play an A chord."

The children all positioned their fingers on their fret boards, and Robyn tried to follow where their hands were. Bryn stood behind her and slipped his arm round her to guide her fingers.

"OK," he said, "4 beats and then we'll change to D for four, and then back to A." He stayed where he was and helped position Robyn's hand again on the change. Robyn tried hard to focus all her attention on the guitar, but it was difficult when he was in such close proximity to her. The electricity that shot through her from the touch of his hand on hers was intense. "Now we'll go to E."

"For heaven's sake," she told herself. "Control yourself." She was both relieved and disappointed when he moved away and picked up his electric guitar.

"OK, let's try that on a loop."

She enjoyed the rest of the class, joining in where she could, and was quite disappointed when it came to an end.

"Thanks for letting me join in," she said to the kids.

"You did OK for a first time," Tom said, sounding very adult for the apparent eight year old that he was.

"Will you come back?" Vicki asked.

"Maybe, if you guys don't mind, but only if it's all right with Bryn."

"It is, isn't it?" Mallory said.

"Of course it is." He shepherded them out of the hall. "Great work, all. See you next week."

When he returned Robyn had put the guitar carefully in its case.

"I'm so glad you came," he said. "I hoped you would but I wasn't sure."

"It was great. You're really good with them."

"They're great kids," he said.

"I had a bit of an ulterior motive as well," she said. "I'm worried about how I'm supposed to find this missing piece. I was racking my brains all day yesterday and couldn't think of anything. I was wondering if you had any ideas."

"My ideas haven't worked so well up to now," he answered. "But maybe a few of us should get together and try and come up with something?"

She nodded.

"I'm free later. Holly and I are busking this afternoon, but after that?"

"I'm working with Julianne, but maybe when we've closed. She might be able to stay for a bit."

"Great." There was a silence.

"Well," said Robyn finally. "I'd better get back. Thanks again."

He smiled again. "My pleasure. See you later."

Robyn felt strangely light and heady as she headed back to the shop. It was a feeling of elation that she hadn't experienced for a while, not since she'd first met Anthony. She allowed herself to enjoy it but that was short lived because as she made her way up the drive she caught a slight movement further along the footpath at the back. Staring intently, she could just make out the huge dog she had seen the other day. This time it had brought a friend. Their eyes burned into her momentarily then they turned and were gone.

Robyn shivered. "Another thing to tell the others," she thought.

Chapter 8

"SO how do I find this missing fragment?" Robyn asked.
She was sitting with Julianne and Bryn in the kitchen after closing. Holly had just left, off with a smile to meet up with a girl who had been to their last three gigs and clearly wanted to find out whether he had talents other than music.

"That's the problem," said Julianne. "No one knows. I think the assumption has always been that it has remained in this area, close to the source, and that when the shield became desperate, it would become apparent. You know, magic calling to magic and all that."

"But it's separate and altered," Robyn said. "It may not be magical anymore."

"There's always a trace left," Bryn said. "It may be too weak to track it properly, but it's there."

"So, again, how do we find it? Just looking desperately anywhere and everywhere isn't working, and we're running out of time."

"Let's try and be logical," Julianne suggested. "What do we actually know that will give us a starting point?"

"Well," Bryn mused aloud. "We know that the fragment is here, in or near the village. All the diviners and seers can't be mistaken, surely. We know that it's likely to be crystalline, and that it may look out of place if it's on the ground."

"We can be pretty sure that it won't be on the beach but further inland." Julianne continued. "The shield was designed to be self healing and self protecting. If that's still true of a detached piece, it will try to find a safe place to stay undisturbed until it can be restored."

"In my dreams," Robyn began slowly, thinking hard, "the only thing I've ever been able to see is the moonlight on the sea. And I'm definitely outside, quite high up I think."

"So maybe the place to start is the cliffs and caves, see if you can find something familiar." Bryn sounded quite excited by the idea.

"Although, the only thing that would give me a clue is seeing where the moon is in relation to me and the sea and I don't fancy going out at night."

"Too right." Julianne was emphatic. "That would be madness."

"But we can work out where the moon would be and go in the day." Bryn was really animated now; Robyn could see he thought she was onto something. "There's got to be something on the internet that'll be able to tell us."

"OK, well, it's too late to go this evening," Julianne said. "So I suggest that you do your research and get some sleep. And then tomorrow..."

"But I'm in the shop tomorrow," Robyn said.

"We are supposed to be in the shop. And I think this is a little bit more important than worrying about working hours. But you shouldn't go on your own, not after that attack."

"I'll go with you," Bryn said. "If you're happy?"

"That'd be great," Robyn smiled.

"Right then." Julianne got up. "I'm going to leave you to sort out your plan. I shall go home and see what my scallywag of a husband has been up to." She hugged them both. "Good night."

"You can use my laptop to look up the moon thing," Robyn told Bryn. "It's upstairs."

She made tea and they took it up to her bedsit.

"Wow," Bryn said. "It's really nice up here." He looked out of the window, watching the comings and goings in the High Street. "Great place to people watch."

"You do that too, huh?" Robyn was logging in to her computer.

"Can't help myself. Naturally nosy. And people just amaze me." He sat next to her on the sofa. "Especially now I know that they may not be human people at all." He lent forward as the internet screen finished loading. "Right, let's see what we can find."

After searching sites for a short while Bryn found what he was looking for. Having obtained coordinates for the local cliffs from the Ordnance Survey site, he put them into the Moon Tracker and carefully wrote down the information given.

"I'm just going to cross check it," he said. "Wouldn't want the wrong directions to stop us from saving the world."

Robyn sipped her drink, part watching the screen and part watching him. With his long lion coloured hair and three silver studs in his left ear, he was about as far from the smart lad about town that Anthony liked to project that it was possible to be. As for the tattoo that curled around his bicep, she could just imagine the sort of derisive comment that it would draw from Anthony. But she liked it. One of the things she had never been able to tell Ant was how much she wanted a tattoo herself.

"I think that's it," he said finally.

"Great," Robyn said. "Roll on tomorrow."

He looked at her and grinned. "Ah, sarcasm, voiced so sweetly I almost missed it."

She laughed. "Sarcasm's the only option, given the circumstances. Actually," her voice became more serious. "If we're looking for a crystal or a stone, how will we know if it's the right one?"

Bryn thought for a moment. Then he dug in his pocket and drew out a small, flat bottle with a silver lid. "We can try using this."

He handed it to Robyn, who held it up to the dimming light. It was full of a green coloured liquid which was glowing brightly.

"What is it?"

"It's something Holly gave me ages ago. It glows when it detects magic. I don't know how it works, it comes from the other realm, but it was another thing he had to convince me that he wasn't lying."

"It's glowing now. Are we in trouble?" Robyn's voice was nervous as she passed it back to him.

"No, it's because of all the protection enchantments on the building," Bryn reassured her. "We're safe."

There was a pause. Robyn shut down the laptop.

"I suppose I should get going," said Bryn, looking at his watch. It was almost nine o'clock. "What time do you want to leave tomorrow?"

"Don't mind," Robyn answered. "Julianne'll be here about half eight, so any time after that."

"Fine." They went downstairs to the kitchen. Bryn swung his leather jacket over his shoulder. "See you in the morning." He got to the door, then paused and turned around. "Actually, I've just realised how hungry I am. You haven't eaten either. Do you want to come over to the Fisherman's with me?"

"That sounds like a really good plan."

As they walked down the road they passed the Anchor. Holly was sitting outside with the girl next to him, his mouth locked to hers. Obviously she appreciated that piping wasn't the only thing he could do with his lips.

"He's such a flirt, isn't he," Robyn observed.

"Wickedly so," Bryn agreed. "Always has been. And he's pretty popular too, as you can probably imagine. But it's tricky for him, given where he comes from. He tends not to get too involved because, well, you can understand how difficult it would be for him to explain who he really is."

Robyn looked back at Holly, who was now laughing and making the girl laugh too.

"I hadn't thought of that," she said.

Robyn and Bryn ended up staying in the pub until closing time. There seemed to be so much to talk about. Robyn was keen to hear about Bryn's time at university, since she had a place to start in the coming autumn; the work, the social life and also the band he had started there, heavier rock than the folk he played here. Bryn wanted to know about Robyn's friends and family, and to her surprise Robyn found herself telling him about Anthony and his despicable behaviour. Bryn looked genuinely outraged and swore, immediately apologising.

"That's OK," said Robyn. "You should have heard what Cara called him. She said..." She stopped.

"I'm pretty sure she said he was something very rude and that you deserve to be treated much better."

Robyn sighed. "Yeah, she did."

"Well she's right."

When the landlady gently ejected them at closing time, Bryn walked Robyn back to the Dragon's Rest.

"I had a really nice evening," he said.

"Me too," said Robyn. She felt strangely shy.

"Maybe we could do that again sometime. I mean after we've destroyed the forces of evil and saved the world."

"If we're still here, I'd love to." Robyn opened the door. "Goodnight, Bryn."

Julianne got there early the following morning to find Robyn packing a small rucksack.

"I've lit the incense, but not the candles, and I haven't put the fairy strands on yet," Robyn told her.

"Thanks. So, what are you packing?"

"Torches, matches, candles, batteries, phone, water, snacks, notebook, pens, salt, nails, red thread, the kitchen sink," Robyn reeled off. "I've still got this horrible feeling that I've missed something important."

"Bryn," said Julianne.

"Honestly, I don't think he'll fit," said Robyn, straight faced.

"Oh, ha," Julianne said, pointing across the room. "At the door."

Robyn turned and beckoned him in. "It's open."

"Hey, guys, all OK?"

"Yep," Robyn affirmed. "I think all that's needed is another cup of tea while you double check that I haven't forgotten anything, and then we can go." She deliberately kept her voice bright, hoping that it would quell some of her fear.

"I'm sure you haven't," Bryn said. "I have every faith in you."

"OK then. Forget the tea. Let's get this show on the road."

Bryn shouldered the backpack despite Robyn's protests. Julianne came over and put salt in their pockets. "Just in case," she said. "Please be careful. And be safe."

"We will." Robyn hugged her. "We promise."

Robyn and Bryn set off down the footpath behind the Dragon's Rest toward the cliff. They walked in silence for a while, both thinking about what was potentially to come. As they came out of the lane of trees onto the field, they could just see the sea to their right. It was already hot, despite being relatively early, the sun skulking behind heavy dark clouds, occasionally forcing a thick finger of light through to stab at the water. Bryn pointed diagonally across to where he knew the multi levelling of the cliffs was most apparent and accessible.

"I think that's the best place to start," he said. "The moon will be over there," he pointed high and slightly to the left. "We can use the different levels for you to get an idea of perspective."

Robyn nodded her approval and they set off again.

"Bryn," Robyn said finally. "What do you think our chances are? Of finding this thing, of being able to stop the damage if we do? I'm trying to think positive but this feels like looking for a needle in a haystack."

"I know what you mean, but honestly, I think you're the key, and I'm not just saying that. Things have changed since you got here, they seem to be much more desperate to find it themselves, and maybe that's because they perceive that we're getting closer. And we are. Before you arrived we were struggling to find any clue. Thanks to your dreams, we've got a great place to start."

"Have you ever been over there? I mean to Holly's world?"

"Only once. It was not long after I found out. The elders wanted to make sure I was trustworthy, so they allowed Holly to take me across."

"What's it like?"

"Initially to look at, pretty much like here. Land, water, trees, grass, small houses and large ones, a market in the village. Geographically it seems similar to here, though not exact. But then you realize there are no cars or trains, and it's quiet, and that all the colours are incredibly bright. And that some of the animals talk, and some things you see are really clear but others seem to shimmer and blur when you concentrate closely on them."

"Were you scared?"

"Honestly, yes I was. Especially when I met the elders. They were obviously very powerful, and they were polite but distant. They questioned me really thoroughly, I guess so they could be certain of my intent. It was quite overwhelming, but eventually they seemed happy to accept that I could be trusted. The offered me some bread, but Holly had warned me that I shouldn't eat or drink anything or I wouldn't be able to leave, so I declined. Then they gave me this pen so I could contact Holly like he contacts me. Holly showed me around a bit and then had to bring me back."

"Why would they offer you food or drink? You'd not be any help to them if you were trapped over there."

"It's a ritual, I guess. Faerie etiquette. Like we tend to offer people a cup of tea when they come and visit." Robyn saw that he was smiling as he said it, and couldn't help grinning herself.

"Yes, I know I'm always making tea. But hey, as vices go, it's pretty harmless."

They were nearing the cliff path now. Robyn couldn't help shivering, remembering the foul little creatures that had attacked her nearby the other day.

"I hope those things, redcaps or whatever they are, aren't still hanging around."

"I would have said it was unlikely." Bryn's tone was comforting. "They like to be on the move. Anyway, this isn't showing any signs of magical activity." He held up the little bottle.

They were nearing the edge of the Overcliff now. Rocks and boulders lay randomly in the scrubby grass, like a misshapen set of giant marbles abandoned mid game. Robyn stopped and looked out to sea.

"Where's the moon?"

Bryn consulted his notes and pointed. Robyn squinted, trying to shut out the daylight and superimpose the silver light on the sea.

"This is partly guesswork," she said, "but I think we're a bit high up. The moon was definitely higher and slightly further to the left."

"In that case, we need to go down here." Bryn started down the steep narrow path to their right, which led to the first undercliff. It was slippery with dust and small pebbles and Robyn almost lost her footing a couple of times. Bryn offered her his hand, steadying her descent until they reached more level ground.

"You didn't slip once," Robyn said almost accusingly. "What are you really, some kind of mountain goat?"

Bryn let out a shout of laughter. "I always wondered why I never really fitted in at school."

"I could do with a drink." Robyn took the backpack from Bryn and extracted the bottles of water. Here." She looked seaward again, trying to judge whether this could be the right place. "I think the next ledge down might be the one."

They made their way down the path hugging the cliff side to the next shelf of land. The ground was stony with patches of salt scorched grasses and a few small but hardy bushes tortured into grotesque shapes by the wind. Cave entrances were apparent all over the cliff, and one opened out onto the area where they were standing. Robyn looked around her from the edge of the cave mouth, judging where the moon would be. A twig caught her arm and made her jump, a memory sweeping over her. She moved slightly, closing her eyes and trying to draw the dream back to her. Reaching out, moving slightly forward, it was all feeling scarily familiar.

"Robyn," Bryn's voice was soft. "Are you OK?"

Her eyes snapped open and she looked at him. "I think this is it. Everything is in the right place and it feels like... like I've been here before. Not in a tourist way but more like a purposeful way, if that makes sense."

"So I guess we start looking."

Robyn put the back pack down by the cave and began to examine the ground. "It would so help if we knew what we were looking for."

Bryn extracted the little bottle from his pocket and knelt down, sweeping it systematically over areas of the plateau. "This is going to be a killer," he said, straightening up and stretching after a few minutes. "Serves me right for being six foot two."

"Here." Robyn extracted the bundle of red thread from the bag. "Tie this round the top, then you can stand up and still search."

"Good thinking Batman," Bryn said gratefully. But after another half hour of fruitless hunting covering pretty much the whole area of the ledge, they still had nothing. Bryn sat down just inside the cave where there was some relief from the sultry heaviness of the air, and Robyn flopped down beside him, disappointed.

"What now," Bryn asked, taking a swig of water.

"Not sure," Robyn said. "We could keep going down toward the beach, check out the next couple of steps. I could have been wrong. I just got such a strong feeling here, but then I s'pose I'm looking for a reaction."

"Instinct's usually the best guide in situations like this," Bryn said. "Why don't we walk down a bit further and then come back and see if you still feel the same."

"OK," Robyn agreed. She pushed herself to her knees, ready to stand, and caught sight of the bottle that was resting by Bryn's hip, still tied to his belt by the thread. "Whoa."

Bryn looked at her. "What?" he asked, following her gaze. "Oh."

He picked up the bottle which had a faint but distinct glow to it. "Maybe you weren't mistaken. There's definitely something here." he said quietly.

"Do you think it could be the missing piece?" Robyn's hopes rose slightly.

"It's possible, but it could be something else. And whatever it is, it's definitely in here, not out there."

"Well, I guess there's only one way to find out," Robyn said, getting to her feet. She got the torches out and handed one to Bryn, who removed the bottle from his belt and refastened the piece of thread so he could wear it round his neck. He put the rest in his pocket and picked up the backpack.

"Ready?"

"As I'll ever be." Robyn's voice was tight. Bryn put his hand on her shoulder.

"Slowly and carefully," he said. "And we stick together OK? No superhero antics."

"Believe me, I'm no superhero," Robyn muttered, but she touched his hand appreciatively. "Let's go."

They made their way gradually towards the back of the cave, sweeping the torch beams over the floor and walls to pick up anything that looked promising. The cave narrowed as they approached the rear, the rock ceiling remaining high but the walls sweeping round and leading into a tunnel. They stopped. The glow in the green liquid remained the same, but when they looked back they realised how far into the cliff they had come.

"This area's riddled with tunnels," Bryn said. "True smuggler's paradise. Trouble is, there's no map. If we go in, we may not find our way out again. But we're definitely on the right track. So the question is, how do we mark our path?"

"We could use thread," Robyn thought aloud, "but it's not very strong, so if it breaks, we're stuffed. I brought some pens, maybe they'd work." She wrestled them from the bottom of the rucksack and tried to draw on the rock, but there was nothing visible. Scraping with the scissors left a slight mark, but the walls were so rough it would have been impossible to pick out their scratches from the many natural imperfections. They stared at each other, stumped.

"Think, think," Bryn told himself. "There must be something."

Robyn suddenly had an epiphany. She fumbled in the side pocket, pulling out a small black tube. "Emergency lipstick," she said.

"Emergency lipstick?" Bryn said. "That's a new one." But Robyn had already made a striking purple mark on the rocks, quite clearly visible in the torch light.

"It works," she exclaimed, delighted. "Blow the diamonds, it's lipstick that's a girl's best friend."

"Here we go then," Bryn said, plunging into the tunnel. It became very dark, much darker than the cave, the torches only illuminating a few feet ahead of them. The tunnel was reasonably wide and still high, and they made their way steadily forward, searching as they went. After about fifty metres the tunnel divided, forking off left and right.

"Where now?" Robyn asked.

"Stay there for a moment, and I'll see what the detector suggests," Bryn said. He took a few paces down each corridor. "Seems to be stronger that way," he said, indicating the right hand path. Robyn carefully marked an arrow back the way they had come, and they set off. This tunnel was narrower and lower, making Bryn stoop slightly. It was slightly longer than the first, opening out into a small cavern from which two other tunnels sped off. Robyn was careful to mark their entrance before she left it. The torch beams looked feeble in the dark, but there was a definite increase in the glow of the detector. Robyn tried and failed to suppress a shiver.

"Are you OK?"

"Just feeling a bit spooked," she said honestly. "It's so dark, even with the torches. It feels like it might just swallow us whole."

"We'll be OK." Bryn's voice was calm. "Stay close. Here." He reached out and took her hand, the feeling of his long fingers wrapping around hers immensely reassuring. They found the opening that seemed to enhance the strength of the green light, marking it and starting into the blackness. This tunnel was narrow but higher than the last one and had a definite downward slope. As they progressed along it they became aware of the faintest buzz in the air, not really a sound but definitely a vibration.

"What's that?" Robyn whispered.

"Not sure," Bryn replied, "but there's something down here for sure. Look." The liquid in the detector was slightly brighter, the glow pulsing as if it had tuned into some unknown frequency. "Let's keep going."

After a short time the tunnel levelled out and opened up slightly. The buzz was still present and the air seemed to be getting heavier. Bryn stopped suddenly, Robyn knocking into him.

"Sorry," she said, but he shook his head and turned off his torch.

"I think there's something up ahead," he whispered. "Can you turn yours off too?"

Reluctantly Robyn snapped her torch off, fear lodging in her throat as the darkness slithered around them. At first it felt like going blind but then she picked out the green glow of their magic detector suspended in the air and Bryn's outline behind it, shadow on shadow.

"Look," Bryn said. "Can you see it?"

Focusing hard, Robyn could see what he was talking about, the faintest glimmer of greyish light apparently emanating from nowhere. She gripped his hand tighter. "Do you think it's them?"

"I don't think it's a fey being," Bryn whispered. "Too still. But it's not earth light, it's definitely something magical. Maybe, if we're really lucky..."

He left the sentence unfinished. Robyn marked the wall and then felt for his hand again as they crept forward. The light was steady but the hum in the air was becoming louder and shadows seemed to shimmer slightly around them. It was hard to move, the air becoming syrupy, a sensation Robyn recognised from her dream. She was just about to tell Bryn when he stopped again and turned slightly toward her. The detector was pulsing madly.

"I'm not sure about this," he said. "I've never seen..."

Suddenly there was a loud crack, almost like thunder, and the ground seemed to tip and give way beneath them. Robyn had the distinct feeling of falling, the walls tumbling away from her although she was still aware of her feet on the floor. It was almost as if something shifted around them, knocking her off balance. She lurched forward, grateful that Bryn had a tight grip on her hand. He caught her as she fell, wrapping his other arm around her until the world steadied again.

"Oh no," she heard him say.

Chapter 9

ROBYN forced herself to open her eyes and the first thing she saw was light. Not very bright, but definitely enough to see by and illuminating the tunnel in both directions. Ahead she could make out the cavern into which the tunnel opened, which also seemed well lit. She looked for the mark she had just made, only to find that it had disappeared.

"Where are we?" she asked. "What happened?"

Keeping his arm round her and pulling her closer to the wall, Bryn let go of her hand and lifted the bottle to show her. It was glowing fiercely now, almost incandescent.

"I think somehow we've crossed over. Into the faerie realm. I don't know how, whether we slipped through a rift in the shield or whether this is a crossing that neither side is aware of, but we're certainly not where we were."

"Can't we go back through?"

"Unfortunately not. Humans usually can't cross unless they're with a magical being, but at the moment everything's in chaos so who knows what rules apply. One thing I do know though, we need to keep moving because somebody is going to be aware of that shift and come looking."

"Which way?" Robyn said. "Should we go back toward the sea?"

"Don't know which way that is," Bryn told her. "The approximate geography is the same but the transposition isn't exact. I need to send a message to Holly, see if he's got any ideas, then I think we should keep going, see if we can find another way out, or something that can help us in the meantime." He felt her shiver and gave her a quick squeeze before releasing her and feeling for the pen.

"I'll mark the wall," said Robyn. "Just in case."

Bryn wrote the message on his arm and they watched it sink into his skin and disappear. Then they made their way cautiously into the cavern which was empty but lit by several flaming torches. There were several tunnels leading off it, most of them also lit. Bryn suggested they take the brightest one, thinking it was the one that was probably most used and therefore the most likely to lead them out. It was eerily silent, their footsteps echoing around them despite their efforts to stay quiet, and they were both on edge as they continued. Robyn marked their way and they walked for what felt like hours, up, down, tunnel after tunnel, with no sign of life at all. Finally they sat down on the ground in yet another small cavern, to rest and eat something.

"It feels like we're going nowhere," Robyn said despondently. "Like in that old film Labyrinth. That girl, Sarah, she keeps walking and walking and it all looks the same, as if she's not getting anywhere at all, no matter how far she goes."

"I know," Bryn agreed. "But we must be getting somewhere, surely. We haven't seen any of the arrows you drew, so we can't have gone back on ourselves."

Robyn sighed. "We need a miracle," she groaned. "Otherwise we could be walking around down here forever." She leaned her head back against the rock. "At least it's not dark. We'll be able to see as we starve slowly to death."

"Cheery, aren't you?" Bryn said. He stretched. "Come on then."

It was then that they heard the sound, a slight scuffling from the tunnel to their left. Bryn was on his feet immediately, finger on his lips. Robyn rose as quietly as she could. There was more scuffling, louder now, voices and a steady tapping. Bryn peered into the tunnel and backed up quickly. He grabbed Robyn's hand.

"Run."

Glancing back as they careered through the nearest opening, Robyn saw with horror a large crowd of small ugly creatures wrestling and pushing at each other. One of them looked up directly at her just before she disappeared. They heard the increase in volume of voices, but didn't wait to find out whether the things had seen which entrance they had taken. They just ran, following whichever fork or tunnel was the nearest. Behind them they could hear sounds, pattering feet and strange nasal grunts and whoops, varying in volume so that it was difficult to tell whether they were being pursued or whether it was echoing through from other chambers. As they exited yet another cavern, Bryn spotted a split in the wall, almost invisible yet big enough to walk through, and he pulled Robyn into the small cave behind it. They stood very still, desperately trying to control their breathing, and waited.

It was a couple of minutes before the noise caught them up. It was clear that the goblins, or whatever they were, had chased after them, following the trail of their footsteps if nothing else. They were in the chamber that Robyn and Bryn had just left, squabbling and bickering about where to go now they couldn't hear anything.

"That way." "No, that way." "No this way." "Stupid, that's where we've been." "They must be somewhere." "Can't just disappear."

Robyn had an idea. She dug some of the salt out of her pocket and nudged Bryn. Holding it up where he could see it in the dim light, she mimed sprinkling it across the opening. He raised his thumb and as quickly and quietly as she could Robyn dropped down and carefully made a line across the narrow entrance. Then she remained where she was on the opposite side from him, sitting half tucked behind a rocky outcrop. The noise in the chamber had reached a critical level, until suddenly a furious roar left them all silent.

"What is this?" the new voice said. "Can I not trust you to do anything?"

"Yes, sir." "Of course, sir."

"Then split up and keep searching. They can't have got far. You lot, that way. You lot, down there. The rest with me."

There was more scuffling and thumping, and then the sound of feet coming in their direction. Robyn drew herself in tighter and she saw Bryn stiffen against the wall. The footsteps were slow, several sets of them, seeming to pause right outside their hiding place. Robyn was frozen, her mouth dry with fear. After the longest minute of her life, the ferocious voice rang out.

"Have you found them, you hopeless bunch?"

"No sir." "Nothing here, sir."

"Well, why are you wasting time? Move on."

At that, the footsteps accelerated past them. From where she was, Robyn could just make out their backs rushing away down the corridor. Small but muscular. She didn't fancy their chances if they had to fight.

They gave it several minutes before they dared move, then Bryn came over to her. She tried to stand up but her knees wouldn't hold her and she collapsed back down in a heap.

"Hey," Bryn sat down beside her. "You OK?"

Robyn tried to speak, but all she managed to get out was "scared".

"Me too," Bryn said. He put his arm around her, feeling how hard she was shaking. "But you saved our lives. Using the salt was genius." He drew her closer so she could lean against him.

They sat together for a while, allowing some time to pass before they ventured out again. It was quiet, and the low light in the cave was strangely comforting. As the adrenaline surge wore away, Robyn began to feel weary. "I could just put my head on his shoulder and drift off," she thought. Out of the blue, she felt Bryn jump.

"Message," he said.

They found one of the torches and Bryn read the words. "Help alerted. Ask the knockers."

"The knockers," Robyn said. "They're the small fairies found in mines."

"And other cave systems," Bryn said. "They're generally really helpful if you treat them with respect."

He stood up and helped Robyn to her feet.

"How do we find them?" she asked. He led her out into the passage and smiled widely.

"We knock."

Bryn used the end of his torch to tap out a rhythm on the stone. Then they stood and waited, listening carefully. A few minutes later, when there was no response, he repeated the call. Again they waited. This time, a faint reply echoed through the rock, apparently coming from behind them.

"Back that way," Bryn said, and they hurried back to the cavern, standing in different exits as Bryn knocked again. A moment later he was shaking his head, but Robyn could hear the answering tattoo.

"This one," she said. And so they slowly made their way through the maze, following the rapping of their guides, until at last they could make out dusty shards of daylight falling across the final cave. Bryn tapped a grateful message near to the opening.

"How can we thank them?" Robyn wondered.

"They appreciate food, bread maybe or fruit."

"No bread left." She took the rucksack from Bryn and rummaged through it. "But I did bring some apples. And what about this? Do you think they'll like chocolate?"

"I'm sure they'll love it," Bryn said, watching as she arranged the apples in a row and broke the chocolate bars into small pieces. "Now let's see if we can get out of here."

They stayed close to the rock wall as they approached the mouth of the cave, not taking their safety for granted. From where they were they could see down across a valley, a village visible in the middle distance.

"I'm pretty sure that's where I went with Holly," Bryn said. "Maybe if we can make our way down there, someone will be able to help us."

"Why don't you try contacting Holly again? He might be able to tell us who to go to."

"That's a good idea, but I don't think we should wait too long for an answer. The light's beginning to fade and I wouldn't want to be out here in the dark."

Bryn was reaching for his pen when there was a sudden loud hum and something large flew into the cave. Robyn instinctively threw her hands in front of her face while Bryn scoured the darkness behind them. The thing came toward them again, swooping round their heads, its wings causing enough of a breeze to lift Robyn's hair.

"What is it?" she panicked.

"I'm not sure, it's so fast I can't get a good look. Hang on." She heard Bryn move across the cave and the hum quietened. Then he started laughing. She peeked out between her fingers. "It's Silver."

Robyn got up and crossed to where Bryn was stroking the dragonfly's head.

"You're so big," she breathed. Silver's eyes sparkled.

"This is her true size," Bryn said. "Her kind did live on earth in prehistoric times but they went into hiding pretty soon after hominids came along. Humans believe they're extinct, but obviously not. Just well hidden."

"What are you doing here, Silver? Did Fiona send you?"

"I think she's come to take us home." Silver gazed at them and they could sense that Bryn was right. "Dragonflies are beings of spirit, they can travel between all realms. And if they choose to, they can help others to cross as well. Will you help us, Silver?"

In answer, Silver fully extended her wings, reaching out the upper set to nudge Bryn on the shoulder." I think she wants us to hold on."

Robyn grabbed the pack off the floor and took Silver's other wing gently in her fingers. Almost before she had time to focus there was a dizzying rush and she found herself sprawled on the ground by a tree that had a massive split in its trunk. She recognised it as the smaller sister of the great oak that she had visited before, out in the woods not too far from the village. She could see Bryn a short distance away, scrambling to his feet. Above them Silver was dancing, back to her tiny size.

"Thank you," Robyn said. Silver flittered away and Robyn propped herself into a sitting position, arms wrapped round her knees. "Are we really back?" she asked.

"We certainly are," he said with relief. "And just look where we landed."

Robyn roused herself and stood up. "I know. The woods. How did we end up here?"

Bryn looked at her, his eyes glinting. "The tunnels must run all this way inland from the cliffs. I knew it was a smuggler's dream around here."

"I'm sure it was," Robyn felt exhausted now. "I think we should go back to the shop and make sure Holly and the others know we're OK."

"You're right." Bryn took hold of her shoulders, turning her to face him. "You were amazing today. We would have been goblin fodder if it wasn't for you."

Robyn shook her head. "You saw them first. If you hadn't goodness only knows what would've happened." She felt sick at the thought.

"Well, we're both OK and that's what counts." He took her hand again as they walked back across the field, and it felt good.

Chapter 10

IT was gone seven by the time they got back to the Dragon's Rest, and Fiona, Julianne, Jim and Holly were all sitting round in the kitchen.

"Thank heavens," exclaimed Julianne as they stumbled through the door. She leapt up and grabbed Robyn in a fierce hug, followed by Bryn.

Holly stood and put his hand on Bryn's shoulder. "I am so glad to see you."

Bryn grasped his other hand in greeting. "You too."

"Are you both OK?" Fiona asked. "Any healing required? Silver let me know that you were back but she didn't say if either of you were hurt."

"I think we're all right," Robyn said. She dropped into Julianne's recently vacated chair. Holly made way for Bryn, while Jim went and found a couple of stools in the storeroom. Over tea and toast Bryn and Robyn related what had happened.

"I still don't understand how we got there in the first place," Bryn reiterated. "If it is a gap in the shield that we fell through, it's a real worry. The thing is breaking down faster than we thought."

"I must speak to the Elders and see what they know," Holly said. "The incursion of non magical beings will've been detected by both sides over there, but I don't know if any of them realise the significance of the visitors." He stood up.

"Go safely," Bryn said.

"Yes, please be extra careful. And pass on our appreciation to our helpers," Robyn added. Holly smiled at her.

"I will, but I'm quite sure they know already."

Fiona left shortly after Holly. The others sat for a while longer until

Robyn could no longer stifle her yawns. "I'm sorry," she said. "I'm so tired I could sleep for a week."

"Me too," Bryn agreed.

"Will you be OK here alone?" Julianne asked Robyn. "Would you like me to stay?"

Robyn looked round at her friends. They gave her a strength she hadn't thought possible. "I'll be fine," she said. "But thanks anyway."

"Do you want to kip at ours," Jim asked Bryn. He nodded.

"Yeah, thanks, that'd be great."

"The building's well protected," Jim reassured Robyn. "You're absolutely safe. Just salt the doorway after we've gone." He hugged her firmly. So did Julianne.

"Don't even think about setting your alarm tomorrow," she said. "Jim and I will be opening up." Robyn opened her mouth to argue then shut it again. She was too tired.

She followed them over to the door, waving Jim and Julianne good night as they left. Bryn stopped in the doorway. "Good night," he said.

"See you tomorrow," Robyn replied.

He hesitated. "Could I have one of those hugs?" he asked.

Robyn moved in to him, and he pulled her close, his arms sliding round her to hold her tightly. Her arms slipped round his waist in response. "I'm so glad you're OK," he whispered into her hair. When they pulled apart several minutes later they didn't need to speak.

Once Bryn had gone, Robyn poured a thick line of salt across the threshold, and made her way upstairs. Although she felt grubby and sticky she hadn't the energy to do anything about it. She changed into her pyjamas and crawled into bed.

A couple of days later Robyn was minding the shop on her own. It had been quiet but she and Julianne had been thankful for that during the morning. Julianne had left at lunchtime to go into Newquay with Jim. It was a muggy day, dark sunshine with towers of heavy grey cumulus threatening from inland. There had been the odd distant rumble of thunder but no sign of the promised storm. Robyn wasn't sorry it was quiet. She was feeling listless and distracted, and much as she usually loved chatting to the customers, she was glad that she could focus most of her attention on unpacking and processing some of the new stock. It was soothing, sitting with the quiet music playing and the incense burning, while clients chatted and discussed the items on display, the soft twinkling sound of the wind chimes gentle as people moved around the shop. She had almost zoned out into her own private world when she became aware of an unusual quietness. The wind chimes had all gone still.

Robyn looked up to see a very tall man dressed in a black suit enter the shop. Apart from his height there was nothing particularly extraordinary about him, but something set off warning bells in the back of her mind. She continued to empty the new box of candles she had just opened, surreptitiously keeping watch on him from the corner of her eye. He was looking around just like any other person would, but she was certain that there was more purpose to him being there than merely browsing. A definite chill filled the shop now. She noticed that the other customers were beginning to leave, slowly but surely driven out by the air of malevolence that was edging through the place.

Robyn gathered up some of the candles and took them over to the stand, fitting them into the empty slots. The man was only a few feet away from her but she could feel the hairs on the back of her neck stand on end. She was as sure as she could be that he was fey. And not on her side. She realised that there was only one other customer left, absorbed in the book section and knew that she had to do something quickly. She did not want to be left on her own with him. Crossing back to the counter, she ducked down behind it and dashed off a text which she sent to Fiona and Bryn. "Danger, shop, come quick" was all it said.

"Excuse me," said a thin voice above her. "Are you the proprietor of this emporium?"

Robyn looked up into the coldest eyes she had ever seen. They were just about blue, but the blue of Arctic ice floes and freezing winter skies. She stood up.

"No, but I'm the holiday assistant," she said. "Is there something that I can help you with?"

"Perhaps," he replied. "I am looking for an artefact, something rare and beautiful. Crystalline, with a sheen."

"Well, we have a great selection of crystals over on the table there." Robyn was not going to let on that she knew exactly what he was looking for. "Tiger's eye, moonstone and goldstone all have a gorgeous sheen. There are also some nice pieces of mother of pearl. Is it a gift?"

"You might say that, yes."

"It may also be worth your while looking at the items in here." She indicated the display case by the door. "There are some exquisite crystal carvings and jewellery."

"I will come back to you if I cannot locate anything... suitable," the man said. He turned back to the crystal display, lifting handfuls of them out of the baskets and allowing them to fall back through his fingers like rain.

Robyn shivered. "Come on, come on," she sent out a silent plea to Bryn and Fiona. She touched the salt in her pocket but she was pretty sure it would have almost no effect on him. He emanated too much power. To keep her hands busy, she lifted a new box of tiny crystal fragments onto the counter and began to fill the small glass bottles in which they were sold. Minutes went by feeling like hours, and she tried not to watch him as he systematically worked his way through the baskets. She thought she detected a flicker of distaste on his face as he handled the haematite, and the clicking of the stones falling down on top of one another set her teeth on edge. A distant rumble of thunder made her jump.

"Get a grip," she told herself crossly.

He came back over. "Be kind enough to open the cabinet," he said. "I still have not found what I require."

Robyn took the key and unlocked the glass doors, retreating as quickly as she could.

"Where are you, Bryn?" she whispered under her breath.

The man went through the cabinet carefully handling everything crystalline. Robyn felt a little better when two youngsters came through the door, her spirits falling when she heard an adult voice calling them away. Then to her complete dismay the man who had been engrossed in the books came over to make his purchase. She served him and watched him leave with a growing feeling of dread. The sound of rain was apparent as the outside door opened and closed.

The man placed the last two figurines back in the case and returned to the counter. "I have not found it, and yet I was assured that the gem I desire is here. Perhaps you have others in your store room."

"All the crystals we have are on display," Robyn said, glad she had fastened the folding part of the counter shut. It wouldn't hold him off for long, but it was better than nothing. "Except for these." She indicated the box on the desk. Thunder rumbled again.

"Where are you, people?" Robyn thought helplessly. "You know you want to shelter from the rain."

"Those are not of the correct size," he said. "You are not being very helpful. I think I will look in your store room for myself."

"I'm sorry sir, but only staff are allowed in the store room," Robyn said. She put a brave face on her terror. He fixed her with a stone cold stare.

"I think you will let me through." He made a tiny closing motion with his hand and Robyn felt a tightening around her throat. "It would be in your best interests." Another movement and she was really feeling the restriction. She put one hand up to try and ease it, the other reaching frantically along the counter for the metal goblet that held some glass beads. "Hmm. Clever girl. You recognise what I am. But iron will not help you I'm afraid."

The tightness was almost unbearable now. Robyn could hardly breathe. She staggered back against the wall, watching as he reached over the counter to find the lock which released the swing section. There was an almighty clap of thunder right overhead as the lock released and he swung the counter open.

Robyn felt as though she was about to pass out, dots raining before her eyes but she staggered forward to collapse in the doorway and try to block his path. At that moment there was a breeze from the shop entrance and the sound of the door. A group of very wet tourists piled in with Fiona amongst them. The man instantly changed his demeanour.

"Are you all right my dear?" He continued forward and offered his hand. When she didn't take it he bent down and half lifted, half hauled her up. "You seem to have been taken poorly."

"I'm fine," Robyn said, wrenching her arm away from him.

"I will be going then." He made his way to the exit. Fiona, rushing forward to her friend, didn't see him turn at the door and put his finger on his lips. But Robyn did.

"Are you OK?" Fiona asked anxiously, but keeping her voice low so as not to alert the customers. "Did he hurt you?"

Robyn shook her head, collapsing into one of the chairs.

"No, but if you hadn't come in when you did..." She couldn't finish.

"I'm so sorry. I didn't hear the text come in. It was Silver who alerted me."

Robyn sighed. "I really owe her big time. So, do you know who he was? Was that Maric?"

Fiona shook her head. "But he was powerful enough to get through the protective enchantments using such a small gap in the salt. There's few who can do that."

A woman from the group came over with some candles and incense. Fiona served her as Robyn was still trying to gather herself.

"Sure is mighty strange weather," the woman said in a drawl from the deep south of the USA.

Fiona agreed. "Don't know what to expect from one minute to the next."

The lady smiled and thanked her. She left with her husband, leaving a few others still looking around. They almost collided with Bryn as he came flying through the doorway.

"Are you all right?" he said. "I'm so sorry, I was further up the coast. What happened?"

Robyn looked up, opened her mouth to tell him, but nothing came out. Instead, despite her best efforts, the tears that had gathered behind her eyes began to spill down her face.

"Robyn, go with Bryn into the back. I'll watch the shop." Fiona nodded reassurance. "Go and have a break."

Robyn didn't argue, just stood up and let Bryn steer her out through the store room and through to the kitchen. He kept his arms round her as her silent tears fell and she was grateful that he didn't ask her anything, just let her weep. Eventually, she regained her composure.

"Sorry," she said.

"I'm sorry, that I wasn't here when you needed help. If something had happened..." The pause finished his sentence for him. "Do you feel up to telling me what went on?"

Robyn nodded. She described the man and his effect on the shop, his search and his attack on her. "Fiona saw him. She doesn't think it was Maric, but he was definitely powerful. I reached for the iron cup when he was trying to strangle me and he said it would have no effect."

Bryn took her hand. "I'm so sorry you had to face him alone," he said. "We mustn't put you in that position again. I'd better let Holly know so he can tell the elders."

Holly came by shortly after he received Bryn's 'text'. He hugged Robyn tightly, his concern crystal clear. "Are you sure you're all right?" he asked earnestly. "Because if you're not, if he hurt you..."

"I'm fine," Robyn assured him. "Just a bit shaken, that's all."

"Tell me as much as you can about him."

"Very tall and thin, dark hair, scary pale blue eyes. He was looking through all the crystals. The wind chimes all went still when he came in, which I'm still not sure how he managed to do with all the spells and things, and he nearly strangled me with just the tiniest movement of his hand. Oh, and he reckoned the iron goblet wouldn't affect him."

"He must be high powered then, maybe even one of Maric's inner circle. I'll see if the elders have any information about him, or how to improve the protection here. There must be a way."

"Thanks, Holly. Be careful, won't you? Will you be safe going over there now?"

He grinned and hugged her again. "Don't worry about me. I'm like a cat, nine lives. I intend to keep them all intact."

"Let us know as soon as you can that you're OK," Bryn said.

Chapter 11

"WE have a problem," Holly said. It was a full day and a half that he had been gone, and although he had let Bryn know he was safe, they had been hoping for some good news. Not this.

"Really? Aside from the fact that we don't have the fragment or know where it is or what it looks like, you mean?" Robyn's voice dripped sarcasm. "Or that we got dropped into the other world by accident because the shield's knackered? Or that malevolent magical beings are immune to the usual charms against them?"

"Hey, it's not Holly's fault." Bryn leapt to his friend's defence.

Robyn sighed. "I know. I'm sorry, Holly. Being scared out of my wits tends to make me act on that old saying 'attack is the best form of defence'."

"It's fine. We're all scared, Robyn, and that's the truth," Holly said sympathetically.

"So what's the problem, the new one I mean?"

"The seeker that came into the shop and tried to attack you, he was obviously aware that there was magical protection laid over it. Rumour has it that he was drained and required intervention to recover when he returned."

"Really? Because he didn't seem to have any bother when he was in here."

"Things are not always as they appear, you know that. Anyway, the issue is that magic can be a bit like a fingerprint. It leaves a trace that is unique to the practitioner. Some of what he detected in here will have been recognised as not from the magical realm. That means that they'll know someone from this side, in our circle, is able to use magic."

"Oh crap," Robyn exclaimed. "Do they know that it's Fiona? Does she know?" Bryn was already on his feet but Holly reassured them.

"I have warned her already, and Jim. I'll tell Julianne shortly. The other side don't know who, I'm fairly certain of that, but we must all be vigilant. There is no doubt that they will come back."

"You have to tell Julianne now," Robyn said. "I'll go back into the shop and cover for her. Bryn, could you phone Fiona. Maybe she should come here. And Jim. At least then we'll all be together."

"Your wits seem to be working very well considering you're scared out of them," Holly observed mischievously. Robyn poked her tongue out at him as she went to get Julianne.

Bryn came into the shop a short while later. "Jim is coming over now. Fiona's still at the market, but she said she'd come here directly she gets back," he said quietly so as not to be overheard. "Then at least maybe we can formulate some sort of plan."

Robyn looked at him helplessly. "I wish I could be as optimistic as you. I feel so far in over my head that I might as well be at the bottom of the Mariana Trench."

"Don't sell yourself short," Bryn said. "You're full of good ideas. You just have to believe that they're good ideas instead of undermining yourself all the time."

"Hmm, well, I think some divine intervention would be a good idea right now. Delivery of the object would be great. If not, a very obvious clue like a big red X marking the spot will do."

Bryn couldn't help laughing. "Given what's gone on recently I don't think even that would surprise me. Not sure what the press would make of it. 'Huge red X appears on cliffs; scientists baffled'."

It was Robyn's turn to giggle. "If that'd freak them out, imagine what they'd make of the goblins." Even as she was still laughing, she shivered.

Julianne came back in with Holly. The moment of lightness that Robyn and Bryn had shared fell away. Robyn had never seen Julianne look so nervous, her usual serenity interrupted by deep anxiety.

"Jim will be here any minute, J, don't worry," Bryn said. "He was finishing the last few minutes of something and then he was coming over."

Julianne gave him a relieved smile. "What about Fiona?"

"She'll be here once she's got back from town."

Jim came in a few minutes later. It was getting crowded behind the counter. "I hate to say it but we seem to have more staff than customers," Robyn observed. "I'm happy to stay here if you guys want to go and drink tea 'til Fiona gets here."

"I'll stay as well," Bryn and Holly said together.

Julianne grinned. "Now then guys, I think you may have to take turns. Who's first?"

The rest of the afternoon passed quietly but by half past four Robyn was getting restless. "Where is she?"

"Sometimes she doesn't get home 'til gone five," Bryn said, putting another cup of tea down on the counter. "It's early yet."

"I'm no good at waiting," Robyn said. "I need instant gratification otherwise I go a bit nuts."

"Well, as long as I can watch." Bryn ducked as Robyn threatened to throw a rock at him. "OK, OK, I take it back. I promise not to watch."

"Grrr," was all Robyn could manage.

When six o'clock had come and gone and there was still no sign of Fiona, they were all beginning to get agitated. There was no answer on her home phone and her mobile was switched off. They closed up the shop and in silent agreement walked along the High Street and into the mews where Fiona's cottage and gallery were. Her little green runaround was parked outside.

"That's not a good sign," muttered Jim.

They were running now, up the path and into the garden, peering through the windows of the house, ringing the bell and calling Fiona's name. No response. Holly and Robyn went to her studio. Worryingly, the door was ajar but there was no sound coming from within. Peering in, they were faced with nothing short of wreckage. The potter's wheel was lying on its side, with ceramics and clay everywhere. Pots of glaze and paint were scattered about the floor, some punctured and leaking. The canvases that Fiona had been working on were torn to ribbons. Robyn's hand flew to her face in horror. Holly's face was set in a grim stare.

"We're too late."

"Oh, no," Robyn groaned. She moved further into the workshop, surveying the mess. "It's a disaster in here. I hope she's not hurt... or worse."

"Maric needs her alive and functional," Holly said. "They won't hurt her. They need to find out what she knows, and when they discover that she doesn't know where the fragment is, they'll try and use her to bargain for the person that does."

"If only they knew," Robyn muttered.

"At least it means she's safe, relatively speaking, for now."

Bryn came to the door. "There's no sign of her in the house, Julianne had her key and..." His voice faded as he came into the studio. "Hell's teeth."

"They've taken her," Robyn said. "But she put up one heck of a fight."

"I'm going back to the elders," Holly said. "See if they've heard anything. I'll let Julianne and Jim know on the way. Meet you back at the shop as soon as I can."

"OK," Robyn said. Bryn was still speechless. They both walked slowly through the workshop, looking at the destruction.

"I hope she's OK," Bryn whispered. Robyn touched his arm.

"Holly reckons they need her too much to hurt her." She gained a half smile in response. "Hey, what's that noise?"

Bryn listened for a moment. "I can't hear anything."

"I'm sure I could hear..."

Just at that moment Jim and Julianne came rushing through the door. Julianne's gasp of horror was clearly audible. Jim put his arm round her shoulders as she stood there, hands covering her mouth in horror. Bryn crossed back over to them.

"If they do anything to her I'll..." Julianne's voice had a hysterical edge. "All her beautiful creations, destroyed."

"Holly thinks she's safe for now, they need her for information. Robyn, what are you doing?"

Robyn had been continuing to track the faint sound she had heard and was over by Fiona's desk. "Hang on," she said, holding up her hand for quiet. "It's definitely over here somewhere. Under here." She ducked down to look under the desk. There was a low pitched buzz emanating from an overturned pot, which she carefully drew towards her. "It's in here."

Jim stepped forward. "Robyn, wait. You don't know what's in there."

But Robyn was kneeling down with her head almost on the floor. She carefully lifted the rim of the pot so that she could see in. Sighing with relief, she lifted the container.

"Silver," she breathed.

Fiona's familiar whirled away from the floor and swooped around their heads before flying out of the door. Robyn stood up and went to the window. The others had followed Silver out, and they all watched her flittering round the garden. Bryn came back in to stand by Robyn.

"Good call," he said.

Silver came back into the studio and flew a couple of circuits round the room before heading into the garden again and back and forward over the pond.

"She's looking for Fiona," Bryn said, as the dragonfly swooped back into the studio. This time she flew so low over Robyn's head that Robyn felt her hair move from the downdraught from her wings.

"Actually," Robyn said. "I think she wants us to follow her."

At that, Silver wheeled around and flew out of the door. She hovered outside the window.

"Looks like you might be right," Bryn said.

"Come on then." Robyn headed outside after her.

As they appeared in the garden, Silver had already moved to the gate in the back fence.

"We think she may be able to track Fiona," Robyn told the others. "She seems to want us to go with her."

"We were supposed to meet Holly at the shop," Jim said.

"Robyn and I can go," Bryn said. "No offence, but we may be a little quicker than you guys. We don't want to waste any time."

"What if he's got some new information?" Julianne asked.

Robyn pointed to Bryn's stomach. "He can always do that transdimensional texting thing."

Silver came back and buzzed round them impatiently. "OK," said Julianne. "Be careful."

"Right, Silver, let's go," Bryn said and they took off at a run out of the gate and along the green lane at the back. Skirting round the copse of birch at the end they were soon pelting across the fields. Silver flew so fast they almost lost her twice.

"Silver, slow down a bit, please," Bryn puffed.

Silver obliged but the change in pace was minimal and they were soon crashing through the woods.

"If we survive this, I'm going to be so fit," Robyn gasped, as much to herself as Bryn. "I've never done so much exercise in my life."

"I've got a horrible feeling I know where we're going," Bryn said, and he was right. In a few moments they were by the split tree trunk. Silver dived straight in and vanished but Robyn and Bryn stopped for a moment to get their breath back and take stock.

"We're woefully equipped to go back in there," Bryn said. "We've got no torches or anything. I don't suppose you've got an emergency lipstick this time."

"No," Robyn confirmed. "We're going to have to go back."

Silver came whizzing out of the tree to see where they were.

"We won't be able to see in there, we need to go back and get..." Bryn stopped as Silver flew into the darkness of the tree and began to glow the colour of moonlight. "So that's why she calls you Silver."

Silver plunged back down into the tree. "Oh well, onward and upward," said Bryn, following her.

"Or downward," Robyn said as she jumped down into the cave after them.

For a small thing, Silver cast a fair amount of light and they could see quite clearly as they took off after her down the tunnel. The first few tunnels and turns were fairly straight forward and easily remembered but then they found themselves in a cavern with four other tunnels coming off it. Silver swooped round quickly and then set off down the one directly opposite them.

After a while Robyn gave up trying to remember the turns they took and just concentrated on the dragonfly who barely seemed to hesitate. The tunnels were eerily quiet, just the sound of their footsteps echoing dully around them. They seemed to have been walking for ages when Silver slowed and came back to them, landing on Bryn's shoulder and extinguishing her light in warning. Robyn and Bryn froze, pressed against the wall, and listened hard.

They could just about hear the sound of feet pounding along, with scornful laughter and jeering. It was difficult to make out where it was coming from but it seemed to be ahead of them and fading in and out as if changing direction. Eventually it became considerably louder and they could discern the clanking of metal and an odd scraping, thumping noise. Gradually it diminished, and the shouting receded back the way it had come until they were left in silence again.

After a few moments Silver lit up again and headed down the tunnel.

"Well done Silver," said Bryn. "That sounded horribly like our friends from yesterday." They continued after her for a little while longer and then her flight pattern changed. She flew low to the ground, back tracking frequently as if searching for something. Eventually she stopped, circling repeatedly over the same area.

"What have you found?" asked Robyn, starting to go over to her. But Bryn put his hand on her arm, stopping her.

"Hang on a minute, I've got a funny feeling about this," he said. "Silver, could you dim your light please so I can see."

"That's some paradox," Robyn thought, but as Silver's light diminished she understood what Bryn meant. A sickly grey glow, just like they had seen yesterday trickling through the gap that had allowed them to slip into the faerie realm, was clearly visible. "Oh," she said.

"So the question is, which side was that sound coming from? And which side are they keeping Fiona on?"

Silver continued to hover. "I would suggest over there, judging by Silver's reaction," Robyn observed. "But how do we find out without getting sucked across?"

"Silver, is it safe for you to cross over and find out if Fiona's there? And come back to let us know?"

Silver's answer was to plunge through the gap, leaving them with only the dull glow. Bryn reached out and found Robyn's hand. "We stick together," he said.

It was only a couple of moments later that they heard Fiona's voice. "Oh my goodness Silver, is that you? How did you find me?"

"Oh, thank heavens," said Robyn.

"Fiona, are you OK?" Bryn called.

"Bryn. I've never been so glad to hear a friendly voice. How did you know where to look for me?"

"Silver led us to you," Robyn said. "Our problem is, we're still in the human realm and you're in the faerie. Hopefully she can bring you out like she did with us the other day."

"Robyn, you're there as well." The relief was clearly audible in Fiona's voice. "Silver, please can you take me to them."

They waited but nothing happened. "There seems to be a problem," Fiona said. "I don't know if it's because I'm too close to the rift but we're not going anywhere."

"Maybe she could take you out to the woods and come back for us," Robyn suggested.

"Unfortunately not. She can only transfer directly to the same place or very nearby. And I can't move."

"Right. Well there must be a way to get you out of there. We just have to work out how. "

"Yes," said Bryn. "How, without being pulled over ourselves and getting stuck."

There was silence as they all contemplated the problem. Then Fiona's voice came up through the floor. "Have you got any rope or string or anything like that?"

"No," Robyn said, but Bryn paused, searching through his jeans pocket. He drew out the bundle of red thread that they had used the day before. "Actually, we've got some embroidery thread. Is that any good?"

"Perfect," came the reply. "If a human wants to cross and get back they need to stay connected to the original side. So you each need to attach an end to yourself and then one of you can come over and cut these ropes they've tied me up with." There was a pause. "That is, if you're happy to."

"Of course." Bryn spoke for both of them. "That's why we came. To get you out." He was trying to untangle the thread. Robyn took it from him gently.

"Silver, could we have some light up here please?" When she obliged they managed to get the thread untangled and rewound. Robyn tied one end securely round Bryn's belt loop and the other was fastened to her bracelet.

"Right," Bryn said, heading for the gap. This time it was Robyn's turn to stop him.

"No, let me," she said." I'm smaller and lighter and we might need you to help us out of there." Bryn looked unsure but she was insistent. "Really, I'll be fine."

"I don't like it," he said, but she could see that he realised what she'd said made sense. She started over toward the light.

"Hang on," Bryn said suddenly. "Silver, do you know how close I can get without being drawn through." Silver came away from the gap about a quarter of a metre which Robyn marked with some stones. "Great, that's closer than I thought."

"Wish me luck," Robyn said. She approached the gap cautiously. "How do I...?"

"Good luck," said Bryn, but she had already disappeared.

Chapter 12

ROBYN felt as if she was falling head first but she landed on her feet in a small cave that was lit by two candles mounted in holders on the wall. The cave entrance had been blocked with a massive pile of small rocks. Fiona was sitting in the corner, hands and feet bound with thick rope. Robyn flew over to her, hugging her hard before starting to work on her bindings.

"Are you OK?" Bryn's voice echoed eerily from the ceiling.

"Fine," Robyn called. The ropes were thick and tightly tied but her persistent fingers managed to work the knots loose. Eventually Fiona was free, rubbing her ankles gratefully with her right hand. Her left hand remained in her lap, forming a distinctly odd angle with her wrist.

"Oh no," Robyn said. "You're hurt."

"I think it's broken," Fiona agreed. "But it's not life threatening. We need to get out of here."

Robyn helped her up and they hurried over to the rift. The problem was, they were both too small to reach it.

"If we jump it should pull us through," Robyn said.

"Unfortunately it doesn't work like that," Fiona said. "We're non magical so the magic only pulls one way. I can't use magic in this realm. We need someone to pull us out. Bryn, did you get that?"

"I would have done more weights if I'd known," came the reply.

"Blinking cheek. So what are we going to do?" Fiona asked. Robyn was looking around.

"Hang on, I've got an idea," she said.

"Is everything all right down there?" Bryn asked. "'cos you know I can't see either of you."

"We're not tall enough to reach the opening," Fiona said. "But I think

Robyn's got a plan."

Robyn was busy gathering the rocks that lay loose around the blockade. She brought them over and arranged them as a base under the gap, gradually piling them up to form a solid platform. Fiona was hampered by her injured arm but did what she could to help position and stabilise the stones. It took quite some time but eventually the tower rose up about four feet. Robyn scrambled to the top and reached up. She could just about get her finger tips through the gap. She helped Fiona up to the top, and continued to bring more rocks over, which Fiona positioned with her feet.

"Not much longer," Robyn said, tugging at a stone that was slightly more firmly wedged. At that moment they heard the unmistakeable noise of goblins scoffing and arguing and coming toward them.

"Robyn, hurry," hissed Fiona.

Robyn gave a last tug on the rock which gave way and came free, loosening others that tumbled into the cave at her feet. It must have also caused a slide on the outside because there was an angry shout, running and the sound of stones being thrown aside.

Robyn threw herself up the tower, putting the last stone in place. She helped Fiona onto it, steadying her as best she could.

"You need to hold onto this," she said, indicating the red thread. "Can you manage?"

Fiona nodded, linking her arm round the thread. "OK Bryn, Fiona's coming through but her left arm's broken so be careful."

Fiona reached up through the gap. Robyn squatted as best she could, getting hold of Fiona round the legs and lifting with all the power she could muster. "Got you," Bryn said, and Fiona began to rise steadily until she disappeared through the rocky ceiling. Just as her feet vanished, the goblins broke through their wall across the entrance and came flying into the cave. They made a beeline for the tower, tearing stones away in an effort to bring it down. Several climbed towards her, swiping at her with sticks to try and knock her off. She kicked out, dislodging two of them, but another two were already starting up toward her again.

"Robyn, where are you?"

"The goblins are through," she yelled. "They'll have me if I stand up."

"Hold on."

Something flew past her face and down toward the goblins, surprising the two that were nearest so much that they lost their grip and tumbled off the tower. Robyn realised that it was Silver, larger than she was in the human world and shining fiercely. She proceeded to dive bomb the goblin crowd who scattered in all directions, apart from a tenacious few who continued to pull rocks from the mound. Robyn stood up quickly and reached up just at the moment the tower slipped. She teetered and nearly fell, just about able to retain her balance. Jumping as hard as she could, she managed to get hold of the edge of the rift with both hands. With a huge rumble the pile collapsed, sending rocks and goblins flying.

"Robyn. What's happening?"

"I can't pull myself up," she cried. "And the tower's gone."

"OK, hang on. Fiona, are you set back there?"

"Yep, go ahead."

Robyn felt her fingers beginning to lose their grip on the stones. "Bryn, I'm slipping," she yelled desperately. Bryn's hand closing round her wrist was the best feeling on the planet.

"I've got you." He reached his arms one by one through the gap, sliding them along hers to grip near her shoulders and then moving slowly back to lift her up through the gap. When she was finally through, he drew her quickly into the safe zone and held onto her tightly.

"All safe Silver, thanks," Fiona called, and her familiar reappeared instantly through the breach, swooping round them in delighted loops.

"We need to get out of here," Robyn said. "I wouldn't want to be around when that lot come through."

"They won't come after us until they've been told to. They're too busy fighting each other to think for themselves. Still, best be on the safe side. Can you show us the way Silver, please?"

They set off after the bright glow that danced along in front of them. Bryn kept hold of Robyn's hand as they hurried back through the tunnels and it didn't seem to take too long to get back to the tree. Bryn scrambled up and helped the others out. Darkness was falling over the woods but it was good to breathe fresh air.

"Thanks, Silver," Bryn said. The dragonfly bobbed in response and then darted away, her glow fading.

"Come on," said Robyn. "Let's get back to the shop. Fiona, can you manage? You look a bit pale."

"I'm fine, thanks."

They walked as quickly as they could back to The Dragon's Rest. The light was on in the kitchen and they saw Julianne's worried face through the window in the door as they opened the gate. The door flew open and she came bowling out, grabbing Fiona in a big hug.

"Oh, thank goodness they found you," she exclaimed.

"She was in the tunnels on the other side," Bryn said.

"And her wrist is injured, probably broken," Robyn added.

"OK, J, put her down," said Jim. "She needs to sit."

Julianne helped her friend into the kitchen, where Fiona dropped into the nearest chair.

"You're so pale," said Julianne. "What can we do?"

"I think I might need some painkillers," said Fiona. "I don't usually take them but my hand is really sore."

Jim retrieved some paracetamol and a glass of water for her and Holly passed her a small amber bottle. "Take some of this," he said. "It's a healing draught. It should help."

Fiona took the medication and gradually some colour returned to her cheeks. "Thanks."

"We need to get you to A and E," Jim said.

"I should go and tell the elders that Fiona is safe," Holly thought aloud.

"I think you should wait 'til it's light Holly," Robyn said. "Goodness knows what'll be out there looking for us now. I think we should all stick together until daylight at least. When there'll be people around and it'll be much harder for them to attack any of us."

"That sounds a good idea," Julianne agreed. "Is there any other way of getting the message across to them?"

"Silver could go. Just transfer directly across and let them know, come straight back," Fiona suggested. "I'll call her."

Almost before they could turn round, Silver was at the door and darted off as soon as Fiona had explained what was needed.

"OK, so if we're sticking together, we're all going to the hospital right?" Bryn said.

"I guess so," Holly said.

"So, if I get the car and take the girls, maybe you two could follow on Bryn's bike," Jim suggested. Bryn nodded.

"We'll be right behind you," Holly said. He sounded relieved. They all knew how much he didn't like cars.

The three of them left to collect the vehicles. Julianne slipped into the shop and came back with a scarf which she fashioned into a sling for Fiona.

"Thanks. That does feel better."

On the way to the hospital Fiona told them a little more about what had happened.

"Did the goblins break your arm when they kidnapped you?" Robyn asked.

"No, that was later. Two of them decided I was dinner and obviously I disagreed. Fortunately their lieutenant arrived in the nick of time and gave them their orders. That was when they took me and blocked me into that cave."

"Did you see Maric?" Julianne wanted to know.

"No. I think I was supposed to be summoned at their evening council but fortunately you guys got to me first, for which I will be forever grateful."

"So how did the goblins get to your house unnoticed?" Jim wondered.

"It wasn't the goblins that took me in the first place. It was a couple of those darn shape shifter creatures. I didn't realise what they were because they had shifted to look like Julianne and Bryn. And obviously since I'd just spoken to Bryn and I knew you were worried I didn't think anything of it. They helped me carry my market boxes to the studio. By the time I realised what they were, it was too late. I tried to fight them off but the next thing I remember is being carried through the tunnels like a sack of spuds."

"Shape shifters?" said Robyn. Weird had just redefined itself. She leaned her head back against the seat and closed her eyes, trying momentarily to blank it all out. It didn't work. She let the others talk on, Fiona explaining how they had found her and got her out.

"Not a minute too soon by the sound of it," Jim said.

It was gone eleven o'clock when they reached the hospital. Robyn and Julianne went in with Fiona and after speaking to the lady at the desk they sat down on the plastic chairs to wait.

"It shouldn't be too long," Julianne told the others when they appeared. "The lady said maybe fifteen minutes before Fiona can be seen."

When Fiona was called through Julianne stayed with her and the rest of them went to find the coffee machine that the receptionist had told them was further down the main corridor. They stood with their drinks and updated each other on what had happened. Holly told them that the elders had been unaware that Fiona had been taken, and that their sources of information about Maric were dwindling. They knew that he was still gathering forces, and that the tunnels had become part of his encampment. Many of the fey that had gone in to try and glean information had not been seen since; the few that had returned told tales of torture and death. The feeling was that Maric's army was getting ready to move, whether the fragment had been found or not.

Robyn shuddered. Seeing this sort of thing as a story on a big screen with a tub of popcorn and your best friend was one thing, but being slap bang in the middle of it was another. And unlike most films, life had no guarantee of a happy ending.

Jim told Holly and Bryn about the shape shifters that had taken Fiona. Holly was visibly shocked by the revelation. "They don't normally come over to the human realm," he said. "It's too confusing, too many possibilities to shift into, and difficult for them to maintain the shift."

"Can they shift into anything?" Bryn asked.

Holly looked at him seriously. "Only living things. And they have to have been in the shadow of, or have had physical contact with, the person or tree or whatever to be able to transform into it."

Robyn was starting to feel quite strange, and the thought that these evil beings had been that close to any of them was pretty much the last straw. She was dizzy and shivering with cold. She moved closer to the coffee machine and rested her head against the metal, closing her eyes against the spinning.

"If they switched into you and J, they could potentially look like any of us. They've evidently got closer than we thought. We're going to have to have code words so we know it's really us," Jim suggested.

"That should work, changed regularly," Holly said.

They continued to talk but Robyn was only dimly aware of it. She felt as if she might pass out. Suddenly an arm came round her shoulders.

"Are you OK?" It was Bryn's voice. "No, you're not. You're shaking and whiter than a ghost." He pulled her against him as she tried to speak but her words came out as an incomprehensible mumble.

"Just feeling a bit wobbly." The second time she tried it came out as a whisper.

"Not surprised," Bryn said. "Jim, could you get her some hot chocolate or something sweet? Not sure if it's shock or what, but she's freezing."

Robyn sipped the hot drink gratefully and gradually some colour returned to her face and the shaking diminished. "Sorry guys," she said.

"You have nothing to apologise for," Jim assured her. "We've all had years to get our heads round this and you've had what? About ten days. Yet you're still out fighting goblins like a pro. I think you're allowed the occasional wobble."

Back in A and E they were told that Fiona had gone for an X-ray. Bryn kept his arm around Robyn, positioning himself so that she could lean against him as they sat waiting. "In another situation this could be construed as romantic," Robyn thought wearily, her heart accelerating nonetheless. She suddenly realised that she hadn't thought about Ant for days. And now she was thinking about him she felt nothing. No love, no hurt, no anger, no betrayal, just nothing. And no feelings of disloyalty or doubt either. It was an odd, empty feeling but one that was so far removed from her current situation that she felt no need to dwell on it. She rested her head against Bryn's shoulder and allowed herself to relax a little.

It was a while later when Fiona and Julianne reappeared, Fiona's arm now encased in a cast and in a proper sling. They headed back to the shop to plan. Silver was waiting on the windowsill when they got back, and they were relieved that she had returned safely. Round the kitchen table they quickly discussed the information they now had and having agreed code words, they decided that Robyn, Fiona and Bryn should stay at the shop which was already well protected. Holly would go back with Julianne and Jim to their house where he would be able to reinforce the magical protection.

"There are sleeping bags in the top of the wardrobe," Julianne told Robyn, "and some spare pillows, I think. I'm going to put a note on the shop door saying we're closed 'til lunchtime. We all need the rest."

"Go home safely, won't you?" Robyn said nervously. "And phone us when you get there. It may sound stupid but we want to know you're OK."

Julianne hugged her. "Of course. Salt the door after us."

Once Robyn had secured the place, they headed up to her bedsit, where she wrestled the sleeping bags out of the wardrobe. Bryn gave Fiona a big hug before she settled down.

"I'm so glad you're safe," he told her.

"Me too. Hey, I never really thanked you guys for saving me, did I?"

"You did, but you don't have to," said Robyn. She took the other sleeping bag over to the sofa for Bryn.

"Well, thank you again anyway." Fiona lay down. "You know how much I appreciate it." Half the sentence disappeared in a huge yawn. "I think I'm already asleep. Goodnight."

"Night," Bryn replied. He looked at Robyn, his face concerned. "Are you feeling better?" he asked her quietly.

She nodded. "Thanks. You really helped me earlier." She looked up at him, realising how kind his eyes were. "Sorry to be such a wuss."

"Robyn," he said taking her hand. "You are as far from being a wuss as the Dog Star is from the earth. Do you know how far that is?"

Robyn shook her head, smiling in spite of herself.

"It's pretty darn far and then some," he continued. He moved closer to her, slipped his arms around her. "But then, you're pretty darn amazing."

Robyn put her arms around him, resting her head against his chest where she could hear his heart. They stood for a while before reluctantly letting go.

"Goodnight," Bryn whispered, his mouth close to her ear. "Sleep well."

"And you."

As Robyn drifted off to sleep, the only thing she was aware of was that despite the situation and everything that had happened she had never felt safer or happier than when Bryn had held her.

Chapter 13

ROBYN woke before the others and lay for a while thinking over things. Then she rose as quietly as she could so as not to wake them, and crept down the stairs. With her customary cup of tea in hand, she went into the shop and made straight for the books. She was leafing through her fourth volume when Bryn appeared at the door.

"What are you up to over there?" he asked.

"Looking for inspiration," Robyn sighed. "There must be something I can do to help find this missing piece."

He crossed over to her and picked up her mug. "Refill?" She nodded. "Any luck?"

She shrugged. "Just an idea. From this book." She stood up and showed him.

"Complete Guide to Spell Casting. I think Fiona's already tried spells." He started out into the kitchen and she followed with the book. "Spell to locate magic objects, spell to find what is lost, maybe another one I've forgotten. That was part of how we narrowed it down to the village, but no one could get any further."

"So what if I tried. Casting a spell I mean. If I'm really this person that is supposed to "restore what is lost', which I still have my doubts about by the way, then maybe if I did the seeking I might get a clearer answer."

"Hmm," said Bryn thoughtfully. "You might be onto something there. It's worth a try at least. Do you know how to cast a spell?"

"Not a clue," Robyn said. "But I'm hoping that Fiona will help me."

"Did someone mention my name?" Fiona appeared in the doorway. Robyn rushed over to give her a hug.

"How are you?" she asked. "Come and sit and I'll make some toast."

"Much better thanks," Fiona said. "I slept like the proverbial log. Feel more like a human being and less like a goblin's breakfast this morning."

"Great," Bryn said. "Robyn's had an idea but she reckons she'll need your help."

"What with?" Fiona sat down opposite Bryn.

Bryn showed her the page that Robyn had been looking at and explained what they had been talking about.

"It might just work," Fiona agreed, "but I think we'd need to rewrite this, make it more specific. Have you ever cast a spell before?"

"No. I don't know where to start."

"That's all right, I can show you. We can do it together. Let me have a think about it for a little while."

"Brilliant. Thanks, Fiona."

Julianne came in through the kitchen door at about half past twelve. "Morning all," she said. "Or afternoon, rather. Custard to you."

"Sandwiches," Fiona replied. "So typical of Jim to pick a food related code. How are you?"

Julianne nodded. "Fine thanks. Jim's next door getting the paper. Holly's gone back over to the elders." She noticed the book on the table. "What are you three cooking up?"

"Custard." Jim joined them.

"Sandwiches," Bryn replied.

"Neither of those," Robyn giggled. "Actually it's a plan. Of sorts."

When they had explained the idea, Jim and Julianne were enthusiastic.

"I think you should do it as soon as possible," Jim said. "Anything that'll help to stop all this can only be a good thing."

"We can head back to mine and do it this afternoon," Fiona said. "I think I've got everything we need. But I have to have a shower and some clean clothes first."

"Me too," said Robyn.

"Me three," said Bryn.

"Jim and I will stay and open the shop. Holly said he'd come back later and help you put some more magical protection on your house, Fiona. He did something with ours last night, but he was going to ask the elders if they could do anything more."

"What about Bryn's place?" Robyn said.

"I'm trying to keep my parents out of it," Bryn said. "They don't know about any of this and I'd rather it stayed that way. If they don't know anything, hopefully they won't be a target."

"You can stay with any of us," Fiona said. "If it makes it easier, until this is over."

"Thanks," Bryn said, looking relieved. "That'd be great."

"OK," Fiona said decisively. "So the plan is this. J squared stay in the shop. The three of us go to mine via Bryn's so he can get some clothes, and magically try again to find the fragment."

"Fine," Robyn said, jumping up. "But I'm having a shower before we go anywhere."

Bryn drove Fiona's car to his parent's place and the others waited while he packed a bag and grabbed his guitar. Then they went back to Fiona's. Bryn and Robyn sat outside while Fiona showered, watching Silver flitting back and forth across the pond.

"Do you think she can see the other side through the water?" Robin wondered.

"Maybe," said Bryn. "Who knows what she can see."

They lapsed into silence. Robyn sighed. "You OK?" Bryn asked her.

"Yeah just... it's weird, knowing stuff that no one else knows. That no one would believe even if they trusted you. Like Cara. She's my best friend and we tell each other everything but I couldn't tell her this. She'd think I was kidding her, or mocking her, or that I'd gone nuts."

"It's tough," Bryn agreed. "But it's also kind of a privilege."

"You're right of course." Robyn sighed again. "Privileges can weigh pretty heavy sometimes, can't they?"

Bryn turned his chair to face hers. "This is all going to work out, you know. Somehow it's all going to be fine."

"I really like your optimism," said Robyn. She met his eyes and he smiled, reaching for her hand.

"And I really like..." He stopped as Fiona appeared.

"OK guys, ready to roll?" she said, joining them on the patio.

"Sure," said Robyn, slightly flustered. Bryn was still smiling at her.

"I guess I'll leave you two to it," he said. "Can I use the shower, Fiona?"

"Of course. Towels are in the airing cupboard."

"Thanks." He walked past Robyn towards the house. "Later," he whispered as he went.

Robyn took a moment to collect herself before following him in. Fiona was already in the living room making preparations. "What should I do?" Robyn asked.

"Could you move the little round stone table into the centre of the room?" Fiona was pushing some of the chairs back to the edges. She pulled the curtains. "We need to form a protective circle to do this. That's fine. Now I just need to get a few things and we can start. Make yourself comfortable on the floor over there by the table."

Fiona disappeared into the kitchen returning with a jar full of salt. She went over to the corner cabinet, getting out a metal bowl, incense, a candle, some paper and a pen. She came back and sat opposite Robyn.

"Fiona, you do know that I have no clue how to do this, don't you?" Robyn was starting to feel really nervous.

Fiona smiled. "Don't worry I'll walk you through it. If you can rescue me from goblins you can do this. It's all about focus. First we need to write the words of the spell. Then I'll cast the circle and light the candle and the incense. Allow yourself to focus on the flame and think or speak the words of your intent. You may feel slightly removed from the world but don't worry, the idea is to allow yourself to enter a meditative state. When you feel the time is right, light the paper from the candle and allow it to burn away in the bowl. You may not get an answer straight away but hopefully something will come to you soon after."

"OK." Robyn took a deep breath. "So what do we write?"

"The spell in the book was OK as a basis, but we need to add something specific to the particular search we're making. Let's see. Help me to find that which I seek, the piece that will make the shield complete. I think that should do it. Will you write that down?"

She repeated the words so that Robyn could write them out. She put the pen aside, holding on to the paper.

"Read them through while I cast the circle." Fiona got up, and walked slowly round the table murmuring quietly as she laid out the circle of salt. Robyn read and reread the spell until it ran through her head like a mantra. She allowed her breathing to slow and deepen. Fiona returned to the table and lit the incense and the candle. She positioned the bowl in front of Robyn. "Focus on the flame," she said in a low voice. "Allow yourself to be quiet and concentrate on the words of your intent. You are outside time, safe in the circle. Breathe and focus."

Robyn watched the flame dance and the smoke from the incense rise and curl around it. The words ran effortlessly through her mind and she no longer needed to remind herself of them. She allowed her mind to float with the rhyme, all the while watching the candle flame, the tiny black space at the base surrounded by the yellow and orange curving to a point. Pictures and thoughts wandered through her head and she let them, observing them and letting them go. After a while, one picture was recurring frequently. Keeping the words flowing she tried to conjure other thoughts or pictures, but this particular one persisted. Shortly after that she lit the paper and allowed it to burn in the bowl. "Thank you," she said.

A moment later she looked over at Fiona and smiled. Fiona returned the smile. "OK?" she asked. Robyn nodded. Fiona extinguished the candle and then released the circle. She came over and put her hands on Robyn's shoulders. "Right madam, come into the kitchen and have something to eat and drink while you tell us what happened."

Bryn was sitting reading when they went through. "How did it go?" he asked.

"Good," said Robyn. "I feel a bit floaty though." She sat down.

"Perfectly normal," Fiona said cheerfully. She put biscuits on the table. "Get some of those down you. It'll help."

She made tea and brought it over. "So, did you see anything useful?"

"I saw the shop," Robyn said. "It kept coming back, even when I was trying to push it out of my mind. I can't help thinking that that's where it is. It seems to be the focus for so much activity it kind of makes sense."

"Maybe. Nothing more specific?"

Robyn shook her head. "No. Sorry."

"Don't worry," Fiona said. "It's not an exact science. Something else may filter through later. If not, at least you have more idea where to look."

Chapter 14

THEY met Holly on their way back to The Dragon's Rest. He looked worried, his usual easy smile replaced by a frown and his bright eyes dark. "You look rough," Bryn said after the required coded greeting. "What's up?"

Holly looked around. "Not here. I need to go to Fiona's and reinforce the guard on her house. Then I'll come back to the Dragon's and tell you."

They hurried along the road in silence. Robyn felt the elation of her first spell wearing away, leaving her flat and anxious. The shop was shut; the Js had closed early. That was even more strange.

They sat in the kitchen to wait. Once Holly appeared and was satisfied that they had salted across the door he began.

"We have to be really careful. The elders are concerned about these shape shifters. They could be anywhere or anything alive. So we can only speak freely in a protected space from now on. Here, Fiona's or Julianne and Jim's."

It was a sobering thought. Robyn felt a chill run up her spine as she suddenly remembered something.

"Holly, is there any way they could have got into the shop? And kept their shifted form long enough to stay in overnight without me noticing? Would they have been able to withstand the protection charms?"

Holly looked at her sharply. "It's extremely unlikely. Why?"

Robyn told them about the two butterflies she had found in the window the week before. "I think it was just before the protective charms were reinforced. I don't know how powerful these shape shifters are but hell, if they were in here..." She tailed off.

Holly touched her elbow reassuringly. "Some of them are quite powerful but I think it's highly unlikely to have been them. Even if it was, they clearly didn't find the fragment and no one on the dark side knows who you are, in relation to it anyway. And don't worry, there's no way any of them are getting back in here now."

"But if I missed something that could have put you all in danger…"

"You didn't, Robyn. No one could have foreseen that. Don't worry so much. You'll get wrinkles." He grinned at her, not his usual full on smile but it still reached his eyes. She smiled back.

"So what did you find out?" Bryn asked.

"It's not good," Holly said, serious again. "Maric's somehow recruited the Wild Hunt."

Robyn saw Bryn shudder. It didn't make her feel any better.

"How?" Bryn asked finally. "I thought they extended no loyalties."

"They don't," Holly replied. "But their services can be paid for, if they feel it's in their interests. And clearly having free rein over not one world but two is looking pretty attractive to them right now."

"I've heard of the Wild Hunt," Robyn said, "but I don't really know what it is. And if it makes you two this stressed, maybe I should."

"The Wild Hunt is a group of outlaws, bandits, whatever you want to call them. They have no allegiance to any court, and they don't abide by any rules or codes except their own. Generally they take what they want, when they want. They do make deals, however, with court royalty or elders if it serves them well, and their support can be bought, if the price is right."

"They're basically hired guns," Bryn said sombrely. "And en masse they're pretty much unstoppable. That's why they're still around. Even the faerie courts don't have the power to take them out, unless they all joined forces, which of course they'd never do. So they've had to find a way to deal with them, keep them relatively contained."

"And that's been to let them live as renegades, with an unspoken agreement that certain lines will not be stepped over by either side," Holly went on. "But now the balance has shifted. Maric has his own court and it's the most powerful. He has the most to offer, and they know it. So of course, that's where they'll be."

"What do they look like?"

"Riders on horseback. They wear masks so you can't identify them. The horses are huge and fast and they travel with a pack of dogs, vicious things with a poisonous bite. I think here they're sometimes called hell hounds." Bryn nodded his assent. "You may have seen one, Robyn. That day in the woods, Julianne told us you'd seen some sort of huge dog. The Wild Hunt use them as scouts."

"So is there any word on what they're doing?" Bryn asked.

Holly shook his head. "Maric's forces are still gathering. They're well hidden and well protected, almost impossible to reach. There have been a few attacks on the local court, but nothing organised and sustained. The Council of Courts has requested troops from any court that can provide them, but that will take time to organise. Maybe too long."

"Is he any closer to finding it than we are?"

"Not as far as anyone knows. None of his scouts have had any success. They're still looking, just like us."

"Do the elders think he'd risk coming across to look for it himself?" Robyn couldn't help but shiver at the thought.

"They think it's very unlikely. But he might send one of his representatives again. That would be bad enough."

Robyn put her elbows on the table and buried her head in her hands. "I don't understand why I can't find the darn thing if I'm the one in this wretched prophesy. I still think you're wrong about that, Holly. It makes no sense anyway."

"Of course it does. Everything about you ties in perfectly," Holly insisted, "especially the increased activity of Maric's crowd searching for it since you got here."

"Crowd," Robyn thought to herself. She imagined them more as a ravening horde. She sighed and said "I'm still not convinced but I guess I'm all you've got. So, what can we try now?"

"Well, we're as sure as we can be that it's here in the shop," Bryn thought out loud. "So somehow we need to find a way for you to connect with it."

"And if my dreams have been anything to go by, it must be a crystal. My pockets are full of them every time."

"So let's go into the shop and see if you can sense anything now. Holly, is there anything you can do magically that might help?"

"Not a huge amount without Maric detecting it. But I might have an idea. Come on."

They left the kitchen and went through into the shop. Soft moonlight was filtering through the windows, just enough to cast deep shadows over most of the room. Robyn switched on the small lamp on the counter, as Holly stood for a moment, looking around.

"What are you thinking?" Bryn asked.

Holly spoke slowly, evaluating his plan. "We know that the likelihood is that it's on the table there. But there are so many crystals, communing one by one is impossible. Takes too long and would require way more power than we've got. So I'm thinking, if Robyn can dowse over the table, it should narrow it down. And I can ask the elemental powers for help. They're truly neutral entities."

"That just might work." Bryn sounded impressed.

"Maybe," Robyn said. "But I've never tried dowsing before. I'm more of a Tarot girl."

"It's OK, I'll guide you through it. Julianne won't mind if we use some of her stock, will she?" Holly said.

"Of course not." Bryn and Robyn spoke together.

"So, Robyn, go over and find the pendulum that feels right to you. No thought, all feeling. Bryn, could you get me some water and some salt. I'll sort the rest."

Robyn crossed to the pendulum display, the beautifully set crystal points hanging from their chains or cords beneath the shelf under the window. She couldn't see them clearly, since they were in deep shadow but that didn't matter now.

She shut her eyes and closed her fingers round each one in turn, trying to switch off her logical brain and trust her instinct. She was aware of Holly moving quietly around the shop but she directed her focus to her hands, making herself acutely aware of every sensation as she touched the gems.

When she finally returned to the counter Bryn and Holly were already there, elemental representations laid out ready - a bowl of salt, an incense stick, a candle and a bowl of water. Holly took the pendulum from her.

"Tiger's eye," he said. "Good choice. Now, you need to hold it like so," he allowed the pendulum to dangle from his fingers, "and wait for it to become still. Then you ask it to show you yes and to show you no. Keep your hand still. The crystal will swing in a different way to indicate each."

"I hope I can do this," Robyn worried. She felt Bryn's comforting hand on her shoulder.

"I know you can and so does Holly," he said. "You just need to believe it yourself."

Holly handed the pendulum back with a reassuring smile. "You worry way too much," he said. "Now, relax and give it a try. Do the same as earlier, don't think, just feel. Ask for your signs, get used to the feel of it. When you're ready we'll set up. Come on Bryn, let's give her some space."

They went back to the kitchen. Robyn drew in a deep breath and held the crystal above the counter. As she breathed out she tried to let all her tension go, to concentrate every bit of her on the pendulum. She allowed herself a few moments after it had stilled and then began to speak.

"Please show me yes." She attempted to stay calm and relaxed, while keeping absolutely still. There was a long pause, then to her relief and delight, the pendulum began to move, swinging round and round in circles.

"Oh, thank you," she said. Gradually the pendulum slowed and became still.

"Now please show me no." This time the movement began slightly more quickly, a definite swing forward and back.

"Thank you so much," she breathed. She confirmed her result and then went in search of the others.

"I think I'm ready," she said, her mouth dry.

Back in the shop, Holly arranged the symbolic elements in the directions they were associated with, with the table of crystals in the middle. Then he stood beside Robyn, chanting very quietly under his breath, while Bryn stood on her other side. Robyn was unable to make out what he was saying but gradually she began to feel a lightening in the air, a thrum of energy rising up through her feet and wrapping itself around her. She sensed that Bryn could feel it too. She held the pendulum in both hands and allowed the feeling to take over. When it was time for her to dowse, she knew instinctively. Holding the pendulum over each basket in turn, she asked "Is the stone I need in here."

When she had worked over the whole table, there were three baskets over which the pendulum had given her an affirmative answer. Bryn rearranged the table so they were lined up in front of her.

"That's odd," she said. "I was only expecting one."

"It's not an exact science," Holly commented. "In either world," he said, catching Bryn's wry look.

"That's what Fiona said. So what now?" Robyn asked.

Holly looked at her seriously. "How do you feel?"

"Fine. Buzzing, actually."

"That's the energy from the charm I cast. I don't want you to overdo it and end up exhausted."

"Really, I'm fine," Robyn assured him. "And time is of the essence, right."

"Right," Bryn added in.

"All right then. You need to lay the crystals out and dowse over them individually to clarify. Are you sure you want to keep going?"

"Yep." Robyn cleared a space along the edge of the table and spread the stones from the first basket in a line along it. "Here goes."

Within the space there was no awareness of time, and Robyn carefully dowsed over all the crystals. At the end she was still left with three, one from each basket; a clear quartz crystal point, a green agate and a dark red jasper.

"I don't understand," she said.

"Don't worry," said Holly. "I'm going to release the energy now, and then we can talk about it."

A short time later, they sat round the coffee table in Robyn's room with the crystals and the pendulum in the middle. Robyn fetched three glasses and Holly poured an inch of red liquid into each from the hip flask he was carrying.

"What is it?" Robyn enquired, sniffing it suspiciously. It smelled like aniseed and honey.

"Restorative potion. Very good after concentrated work," Holly said.

"Faerie energy drink without the caffeine side effects," Bryn added, as Robyn was still looking mystified. Cautiously she took a sip, warmth flooding through her veins. It was calming and gently energising. She sighed contentedly.

"You've done really well," Bryn said. "One of these must be it."

"Or maybe all of them," Holly suggested. "A piece was lost, but it could have further broken down. No one knows. We must just make sure they're well protected until they're needed. And we can't tell anyone."

"Not even Julianne?" Bryn said

"Not Julianne, not Fiona, no one. It's too risky. The shop is cloaked and protected when it's locked but there may be spies everywhere else. The more people who know we have it, the more people are at risk. And the more likely he is to find out and come after it. No. We keep it to ourselves."

"How do we protect the crystals?"

"By putting them in a salt filled bag in a box, iron preferably," Holly instructed. "Have we got what we need?"

"Salt's no problem, and there are those little velvet pouches in the shop. A box, though, I'm not sure." Bryn drummed on the table with his fingers.

"I think I might have one," Robyn said, getting up. She kept her jewellery in a small wooden box which had metal bands around it. "Will this do?"

"If those bands have iron in," Holly said. "Do you know what metal they are?"

Robyn shook her head. "No, sorry."

"Oh well, only one way to find out I guess," Holly muttered. He reached out tentatively toward the box where it lay on the coffee table and gently brushed his finger against the band. There was a spark and he rapidly withdrew his hand, cursing as he rubbed it with the other. "Crap and more crap, that's definitely iron."

"What happened? Are you OK?" Concerned, Robyn sat beside him.

"I'm fine." Holly gave his finger a last squeeze. "But that's why my kind don't like iron. It gives us a shock, like electricity would do to you. If you're careful and prepared you can guard against it to some extent, but let that guard down and... ouch."

"I'm sorry," she said.

"Hey, it's not your fault. And we know this will be perfect." Holly was pleased despite his discomfort.

Bryn retrieved a pouch and some salt, and they secreted the crystals under the necklaces and other bits and pieces. Robyn stashed the box in her wardrobe and came back to the sofa, trying but failing not to yawn. Bryn stood up.

"You look tired now. It's nearly one o'clock. We should go."

Robyn went down to lock the door behind them.

"Still doubt you're our girl?" Holly said, half joking. He gave her a quick hug. "You're a fast learner, that's for sure."

Bryn followed. Rather self-consciously he took Robyn's hand and squeezed it. "You're amazing," he said. "Sweet dreams tonight." He bent down to brush a gentle kiss on her cheek.

Then he disappeared through the door after Holly.

Robyn locked up and got ready for bed, falling into it gratefully. Her cheek tingled where Bryn's lips had touched her. She was still smiling as she drifted off to sleep.

Chapter 15

ROBYN had a particularly dark and disturbing dream that night. She was in the usual place struggling to move and find her bearings but this time there were hands forcibly holding her back while yet more hands searched through her pockets, taking the crystals one by one. The more she fought the tighter their grip on her became, until she felt that she was trapped there forever. "We'll give them to him," the voices whispered. "He will be so pleased with us."

"No." Robyn tried to scream but nothing came out of her mouth. She was straining so hard against her captors that she actually woke herself up with a yelp.

"Oh jeez," she gasped. She sat up, relieved that she could move all her limbs. "That was horrible." She got out of bed feeling really shaken. The dreams had always seemed real but that one had been beyond that. It felt as if they had actually been in her head. And try as she might she couldn't get rid of the sensation of being trapped.

Robyn dressed and went downstairs despite the early hour. She sat in the shop and read, trying to block out the haunted feeling, and was relieved when it was time to open up. She was on her own for the first hour, but the drizzle brought in some early customers and before she knew it Julianne appeared.

"Pancakes," Julianne said, hugging her.

"With sultanas," she replied.

"You look tense this morning. How did it go with Fiona yesterday?"

Robyn bit her lip. "OK. Think we got a bit closer. She thought more info or inspiration or whatever might come later, but I'm still waiting for that." She found it so hard not to tell Julianne about what they had found the evening before. "I just had a really bad dream last night. It really felt like I was there on the cliffs and they were restraining me. I couldn't get away."

"Oh sweetie, that sounds horrendous."

"Yes, well, I'm having a bit of trouble getting rid of the feeling this morning. It's like I'm being watched from inside my own head."

Julianne put an arm around her. "You know you're safe in here right? Not even Maric could get through the magical barricades on this place now."

"I know but I still feel helpless. Finding the fragment's one thing but then what am I supposed to do with it?"

Julianne sighed. "I think we have to trust the magical process. We're so used to science and logic that we tend to panic when we don't have all the answers. But magic isn't like that and sometimes answers come at the strangest and most unexpected of times."

"I hope you're right," Robyn said grimly.

"Try not to worry. I know it's easier said than done."

"You're not wrong there," Robyn agreed.

Although they were relatively busy because the drizzle had turned into proper rain, the time seemed to drag. All the positivity that Robyn had felt the day before had drained away leaving her low and exhausted. It felt hard to function. Julianne was in a quiet mood as well and so they didn't talk like usual, each wrapped in her own thoughts. Bryn came in about threeish. He had been supposed to be busking with Holly but they had cancelled because of the bad weather.

"And now he's done a Holly vanishing trick."

"You could always text him," Robyn said pointedly.

"I'm sure he's fine," Bryn assured her. "Just being his usual capricious self. You look worn out today though. Are you OK?"

"Had a really bad dream," she told him.

"And also you're probably tired from working with Fiona yesterday. I think that can take it out of you," commented Julianne.

"True," Bryn agreed.

"Maybe," Robyn said. She served the customers and let Bryn and Julianne chat. Somehow she couldn't summon up the energy. It was easier to switch on automatic mode and bury her terror and feelings of helplessness under a fake smile and a cheery exchange of small talk.

It was a little later that Holly appeared in the storeroom doorway. One look at his face had Julianne on her feet. He was wet and covered in dirt and he beckoned them all over urgently.

"What on earth's happened?" asked Julianne, trying to keep her voice low.

"It's Oonagh. She's in the kitchen," Holly whispered. His eyes were desperate. "She was coming over to tell us something urgently and she was attacked. It was lucky I was there, but she's injured too badly for my healing potion. I didn't know what else to do so I brought her here."

"OK," said Julianne, thinking fast. "Robyn, can you stay here for a minute while we see what's what. Bryn, call Fiona, I'm sure she can help. Let's go."

The others disappeared out to the back and Robyn was left alone with the three remaining customers. Strangely she felt completely alone. And as if she could do nothing useful to help.

About twenty minutes later Bryn reappeared.

"How is she?" Robyn asked, her gut knotted with dread.

"Not great," Bryn said seriously. "We've taken her upstairs so she can lie down. Fiona knows a lot about healing and she's there now, so I think she'll be OK. She needs to be strong enough to get back to the other side though, where they can heal her properly."

Robyn put her hand over her mouth. "Oh darn. What if she can't...?"

"We'll make sure she does. One way or the other. Julianne said to ask you to close up when these last few have gone. Jim's on his way. We need all of us up there."

Robyn nodded. "I'll be through as soon as I can."

When Robyn made it to her room quarter of an hour later Jim had just arrived. Oonagh was lying on the bed and Fiona was helping her sip something from a small glass. She had cuts all over her face and arms which had been treated with the balm that Robyn recognised. She looked even paler than the first time Robyn had seen her. Holly was standing by the sofa looking completely lost. She went over to him, taking his hand and squeezing it. He squeezed back gratefully, keeping his eyes on Oonagh.

"How is she?" Robyn whispered.

"A little stronger," he said quietly. "It'll take some time but she seems to be recovering."

Eventually Oonagh was able to sit up without severe dizziness.

"Steady now," said Fiona. "Don't rush."

The faerie elder sat on the edge of the bed for a few moments and then rose slowly, walking across the room to the armchair with Fiona and Julianne on either side of her. She sat down again.

"You have made a great difference and I am grateful," she said. "But I must return home soon so that I can fully heal. I had come to pass on a message, information that there would likely be an increased number of crossings in the next few days, so far more danger to you and your kind. I think the risks are now evident."

"What, so this didn't happen in the borders?" Jim asked, obviously shocked.

"No," Holly confirmed. "It happened here, on this side. A pack of redcaps and a couple of hellhounds. We were lucky to escape alive. There seem to be several rifts in the tunnels now which they're utilising to increase the pressure."

Bryn was shaking his head. "They must think they're nearly invincible if they'd dare to attack an elder. Especially here."

"Yes," Oonagh agreed. "And they have become stronger. Maric is using a combination of powers to reinforce all the others. It makes the whole stronger than the sum of the parts and they all seem to be able to tap into it."

Fiona shook her head. "That shouldn't be possible."

"Nevertheless, that is what is happening. We believe that they are almost ready to come across as an army, fragment or no fragment." She leaned forward. "That is why you must hurry. There is a lunar eclipse two nights from now. The likelihood is that they will use its power to help them break through. You must hurry, or all will be lost." She looked at each of them in turn, Robyn last. "I know how hard you have all endeavoured and the risks you have taken. And I know, Robyn, that this is a heavy burden to carry, for everyone but especially for you. You must learn to trust yourself. The elders are sorry to ask this of all of you, but there is no other way. So please, hurry."

"I'll try," Robyn said quietly.

"I must go now," Oonagh said.

"Silver will help you." Fiona walked to the window and almost immediately Silver was swooping into the room. She flew straight over to Oonagh and landed on her arm.

"Thank you." Oonagh looked round the room again. "And fare well." There was a shimmering over her and then she was gone. They sat in shell shocked silence and minutes went by.

"So what now?" Jim asked finally.

"We need to help Robyn find the missing piece." Julianne said. "What else can we try?"

Robyn looked over at Holly, silently asking whether to say anything and saw him almost imperceptibly shake his head. She thought fast.

"Nothing," she said. "You don't have to do anything. I need to do something. It's here somewhere and I need to focus and find it."

"But we can help," Fiona said. "Holly and I can focus our energy with you, it might make it easier."

"No," Robyn said, trying to sound decisive. "This seems to be down to me. I don't want anyone else hurt. I think the best thing is for me to stay and work on it so I can really concentrate, and for you lot to go and do something else. Fun preferably. See a band, watch a film. Get out of the village so you're less at risk."

"That doesn't seem fair." Julianne sounded doubtful.

"It's OK, really. It makes sense. I'd like you all to go and have a good time. You've been doing this a lot longer than me. I need to catch up."

"I don't think..." Jim started, but Robyn stood up and pasted a smile on her face.

"It makes sense, you know it does," she insisted. "I need quiet to focus, so the quicker you lot vacate the premises the quicker I can get started. And I know the film that you two," she looked at Fiona and Julianne, "were talking about is playing this week. So you might as well go and see it."

"Are you sure?" It was Fiona's turn to sound unsure.

"Really. Now let's go. I have some concentrating to do." She began to shoo them downstairs.

"I do believe we're being kicked out of our own shop," Jim said to Julianne with mock indignance.

"Too right you are," Robyn agreed. She kept the grin fixed firmly in place. "Have fun. That's an order."

"So who's coming?" Jim said. "Fiona? Julianne?" They both nodded. "Holly? Bryn?"

"I'll come if I can get cleaned up first," Holly said.

"I'll pass, thanks," Bryn shook his head. "I'll just eat and then probably head back to yours, Jim, if that's all right."

"Of course," Julianne said. She looked at Robyn. "Are you sure about this? It doesn't feel right leaving you."

"Absolutely. Now go, enjoy, and maybe tomorrow I'll have something good to tell you."

"OK," Jim said, as they all hugged her. "Call us if you need us."

"I will. Stop worrying."

They started heading out. Bryn dug in his pocket and pulled out his keys, handing them to Holly. "Take the bike. You'll be more comfortable."

"Thanks." Holly tossed them up and caught them again. "So much more fun too. And better for my image."

Fiona laughed. "Says the king of glamouring."

"See you guys tomorrow," Robyn said. "Be careful."

"What's up?" Bryn asked her when the others had finally left. "You're really on edge."

"Nothing. I'm fine." She walked over to the window and stared out into the garden. He came and stood next to her.

"Really? I'm not convinced. You found the fragment last night. You should be feeling happy despite what's just happened, and you're not."

Robyn felt tears stab at the back of her eyes and fought them down. She was furious with herself. Furious about the tears and furious that he could read her so well and that she had let him.

"Really. I'm absolutely fine. Just bad company, that's all."

"You're never bad company," Bryn said. "I'll go if you don't want me here, but if you want to talk, that'd be OK."

Robyn bit her lip. She wanted to talk to him, to feel his arms around her, to hide her face against his shoulder until the whole horrible mess went away but she knew she couldn't.

"Honestly Bryn, I'm OK. I'm just having a grumpy day. Tired after yesterday and worried about what Oonagh said, but then aren't we all? You'd be better going to see the film with the others."

She pushed herself away from the counter. "You can still catch them if you hurry. I've got to go and tidy up." She smiled at him, not meeting his eyes and wrenched herself away into the shop. She hadn't ever felt as low as she did at that moment. Not even when she'd seen Anthony kissing that girl.

She was retying some of the scarves on the rack a few minutes later when she heard Bryn at the door, but she ignored the sound even though her heart jumped and her hands shook even more. She kept her back to him and focused desperately on what she was doing, even when his steps approached her. Then she felt his hands on her shoulders and tensed, holding her breath.

"Robyn, stop," he said softly. "Please talk to me. Tell me what's wrong."

Robyn was rigid. She exhaled slowly, shaking her head, but it didn't clear all the thoughts that were scrambling like ants through her mind. "Nothing," she managed to get out.

Bryn reached an arm in front of her to her opposite shoulder and gently turned her to face him. He bent down so he could look directly into her eyes. She tried to avoid his gaze but it was impossible.

"We're in this together, remember?" he said. "One for all and all for one. You can tell me anything."

The tears were back behind her eyes. She felt she should pull away but the truth was she didn't want to be anywhere else. "Oh crap," she said, covering her face with her hands. "Bryn, why are you so nice to me? When you should be angry because I'm so useless and I've probably failed everyone."

"Whoa. What?" He tried to pull her hands away but she wouldn't let him. "You haven't failed anyone. You've been incredible. What do you mean?"

"It's like Oonagh said earlier. If we don't hurry, all will be lost. We thought we'd found it last night but even if we have, I don't know what to do with it. And I'm the one that's supposed to know how and when and what, but I don't know anything. I'm scared. I'm lost. You should be yelling at me, telling me to get a grip and get on with it. Not being nice to me." Her voice cracked.

"Robyn, you are amazing. You have found the fragment whether you believe it or not, and you will know how to fix things when you need to. Just because you're the one in this prophecy doesn't mean it's your responsibility alone. We're all in it together." He tugged at her hands again and this time she let him pull them away from her face. "I am in this with you all the way to the end. And beyond." There was so much light shining out of his eyes that the tears welled up again. She brushed one away.

"Oh for goodness sake, please stop being so nice to me," she said huskily. "Or I'll probably cry."

"That's OK," he said, gathering her into his arms. "You're allowed."

Robyn had no idea how long they stood there, how long he rocked her while she cried, but they remained long after her tears stopped. Neither of them wanted to let go. Her arms were locked around his waist, his hands gently stroking her back. She could have stayed there forever but eventually she loosened her grip.

"Better?" he asked, still holding on to her. She leaned back slightly so she could look at him and nodded.

"Thanks," she whispered.

He hugged her again and then released her, taking her hand instead. "Let's go and make a cup of tea." He smiled at her. "And then maybe we could sit upstairs for a bit? Talk. Listen to music. Watch a film. Something?" When she nodded again he led her out into the kitchen.

They took their tea upstairs. "Let's distract ourselves with some rubbish TV," Bryn suggested. "Find something funny. You need a good laugh."

He switched it on and sat at the end of the sofa, flicking to find some comedy. Robyn stood, feeling slightly awkward and unsure what to do. She went to sit down in the chair.

"Hey," Bryn said. "Come here." He reached his hand out and caught hers, pulling her down onto his lap and wrapping his arms around her. "Sorry but I want you as close to me as possible." Robyn didn't argue. She rested her head against his chest and allowed the moment of blissful happiness to envelop her completely.

They talked and watched a couple of programmes that made them laugh out loud. A film started that Bryn reckoned was half decent, so they left that on. But at some point Robyn must have dozed off because when she came to the film was ending and Bryn's phone was beeping.

"Oh, I'm sorry," she exclaimed with a start. She moved to get up, but his arms tightened around her. "What's the time?"

"Half eleven. It's OK. Do you always wake up with such a jump?"

Robyn relaxed a bit. "Since I've been having those dreams. I don't really notice it any more. Your phone was going."

"It's probably Julianne checking up on me." Keeping hold of her, he leaned forward to lift his mobile from the table. "Yep."

"I s'pose you'd better go," Robyn said wistfully, resting her head back down against his shoulder. She kept her arm round him.

"I s'pose I better had." He didn't move, but Robyn could feel the tension suddenly running through him. "I don't want to though. I want to stay here, just like this."

She was still, her heart thundering. "You don't have to," she said quietly. "The place is well protected."

"I know that," he replied. "But I still don't want to go." He moved slightly, tilted her head up so he could see her face. "Would you let me stay, Robyn? Just like we are now, nothing else. I don't want to be away from you."

"Yes." She barely recognised her own voice. "Please."

Bryn relaxed back a little and phoned Julianne. Robyn shifted on his lap so she could see him better, smiling when he grinned and raised his eyebrows. Julianne was obviously teasing him.

"She give you a hard time?" Robyn asked when he finished the call.

He shrugged. "Oh, just told me to behave myself. And to look after you or she'd de-string my guitar and turn it into a garden ornament. As if I'd do anything else. I don't want you to kick me out."

"That's highly unlikely." Robyn stood up.

"Hey, where are you going?" His question was answered when she came back with the duvet from the bed. She turned off the TV so it was just the light from the lamp that illuminated the room.

"It'll be chilly later. We may as well be warm."

He pulled her back down, settling them both so they were comfortable, and wrapped the duvet around them. Robyn was turned toward him this time. She smiled at him, feeling slightly overwhelmed by the way he was affecting her, the way he looked at her. He ran his thumb along her jawline and it made her shiver inside. She looked away, at the tattoo on his upper arm.

"I like that. I'd like to get one, not sure what yet. Does it hurt when they do it?" Her voice was lower than usual.

He continued to stroke her gently, running his hand down her neck to her shoulder and over her back. "You need to be really sure first," he said quietly. "It's a bit sore but not too bad. Nothing you couldn't handle."

She traced her finger along the lines that wound round his arm, trying to ignore the heat that was flooding through her from his touch. "Where'd you get it done?"

"A guy that Holly knows in Newquay did it for me last year. It's Celtic knot work. And if you keep touching me like that I may not be responsible for my actions."

Robyn moved her hand away and looked at him. "Sorry," she said.

"Don't be sorry. Ever." That was when he drew her close and kissed her, kept kissing her until they were both breathless. And then he held her tightly again as they drifted off to sleep.

Chapter 16

ROBYN woke the next morning with her head tucked against Bryn's chest and his arm around her waist. Sometime in the night they had moved down to lie side by side on the sofa. He had evidently woken before her because he was propped up on the arm, looking down at her. He stroked some of the hair away from her forehead as she slowly opened her eyes.

"Hi," he said. She just smiled and he moved so his head was beside hers. "You're gorgeous, you know that, right?" His arm came back around her and she moved hers round him, shaking her head. "Well you should," he went on. "And you looked so peaceful when you were sleeping. No bad dreams?"

"No. Maybe you're my lucky charm."

"Any time. Always." He kissed her again then, and Robyn tangled her hand in his hair and held him fiercely. She wanted to make the most of this moment because they both knew that things might never be the same again.

It was still early when they finally tore themselves apart. Bryn headed downstairs to make some breakfast while Robyn showered and changed. She couldn't believe how she felt with Bryn, how safe, how complete. The way Bryn treated her was certainly miles away from how Anthony had been. She thought back to how devastated she had felt when she had discovered he was two timing her. "If only I'd known," she thought.

They sat and ate in the kitchen, not saying much but unable to stop smiling at each other. Afterwards he said he'd help her tidy the shop. She began to clear the plates away, putting them down when she noticed a spider crawling beside her mug. She picked it up and looked at it closely.

"Well, I'll give you full marks for persistence, missy," she said to it. "But you really shouldn't be in here."

"What've you got?" Bryn asked, coming over for a closer look.

"A garden spider that seems to want an indoor life," she replied. "I keep finding her, or else this is her twin. But really," she said, addressing the spider again, "you need to be out there where you can hunt properly. Otherwise you'll be poorly." She opened the kitchen door and took the creature over to the hydrangeas. "There."

"So how come you're such an arachnid expert?" Bryn wanted to know when she came back in.

"Oh, just one of my odd little ways," she teased him. "That and an older cousin who liked to try and freak me out. I decided when I was seven that I wasn't going to let him. So now spiders and all sorts of bugs and creepy crawlies are my friends. Except wasps. I really can't stand them."

"You," he said, embracing her again, "are very unusual. And that is a very good thing."

She couldn't help laughing. "Haven't you got work to do?" he said, walking her backwards toward the shop.

"Yes, but you seem intent on distracting me," she said, her arms round him to try and keep her balance.

"Oh, so it's my fault you're slacking is it?" he laughed. "Well this is not distraction. This is distraction." He kissed her again. "I'm distracted. How much work have you got to do?"

"Not much," Robyn sighed. She kissed him back. "I've got time for some distraction."

They made sure that by the time half past eight came around the shop was tidy. Robyn opened up. The sky was threatening and there was a chilly wind making the awnings outside some of the other shops flap. She came back in shivering.

"It's not nice out there," she said. "There's something up with the sky. The clouds are a weird colour and it looks like they're boiling, but it's really cold."

Bryn went over to the window to look. "It's not good, is it? I've heard Holly talk about the storm clouds over there. They move like that, almost within themselves."

Panic started to rise. "Do you think they've broken through already?"

"No, I think we'd know. It's probably a reflection, more obvious than usual because the shield is breaking down. It looks like Oonagh was right, the lunar eclipse may be their best chance."

"And that's tomorrow." Robyn's mouth was suddenly dry.

He came back to her and hugged her. "You escaped redcaps and rescued Fiona from goblins. You found the fragment. Fixing the shield will be easy."

"I wish," she muttered. "But where? And how?"

"How what?" Julianne said as she walked in. "Peanut butter, by the way."

"Jelly," Bryn replied. "How was the film?"

"Good. More importantly, how are you two? On second thoughts, don't bother to answer that. I can see by the smiles on your faces that you're fine."

"What about Oonagh? Have you heard anything?" Bryn asked.

"Holly's chanced going over this morning to find out, even though the sky looks horrendous. I think they might be right about this eclipse. Did you manage to find anything, Robyn?"

Robyn winced at being put on the spot. "I think I've narrowed it down," she said. "I took a few bits upstairs, I hope that's OK."

"Of course. Whatever you think will help is fine." She grinned at them. "You both seem to have found what you need though." Robyn blushed but Bryn had a wide smile on his face. He gave her a squeeze.

"I'm going to go back to yours, J, and get changed. I'll see you later." He gave Robyn a quick kiss and was gone.

"Stop grinning at me, J," Robyn hissed at her a few minutes later.

"Maybe when you stop grinning yourself," Julianne shot back. "I knew you'd get on well with him. I just didn't realise how well."

Robyn clapped her hands over her burning cheeks. "Right. I'm going over there where you can't embarrass me for a while."

Fiona came in at about eleven. "Hi," she said to Robyn. "I understand your focus was directed in more ways than one last night." She raised her eyebrows pointedly.

"My focus was just fine, thank you," Robyn replied.

"So I hear," Fiona laughed. "I'm so happy. And how about the other thing."

"Definitely getting there."

"Great. So much better than yesterday's news. I've got to steal Julianne this afternoon, we've got to go into Newquay with Jim to a trade fair. Will you be OK? Obviously we'll all be around tomorrow because..."

"No problem," Robyn said. "Bryn said he'd come back, and I'm sure Holly'll turn up at some point."

"Thanks, lovely," said Julianne. "See you tomorrow."

Bryn came back a while after they left. "The clouds are clearing," he said. "But something definitely feels off. The sky looks as if it's been bleached and though the sun's out, it still feels really cold."

"Gathering storm," Robyn muttered. "If they're trying to freak us out before tomorrow, they're certainly succeeding in my case. Have you heard anything from Holly?"

"No, why?"

"I'm just a bit concerned given what's gone on. He went across this morning and now it's what, nearly half one and he's not back and we haven't heard anything. I just hope he's OK. You know, after yesterday's attack."

"Yeah, but sometimes it does take a while. Still, you've got a point. I'll go and "text" him."

Bryn disappeared out the back. Robyn paced around the shop. It had been incredibly quiet all day and currently there were no customers in. It made her uneasy. Even with the unpredictable weather over the summer there had still been a steady flow of people in and out. Today it wasn't just the sky and the clouds that conspired to worry her. It was just about everything.

Bryn came back through. "He's OK and so is Oonagh. I've texted the others to tell them. He's in the middle of something, he said it'll give us some useful information. He'll be here later."

"I hope he's not doing anything risky. Or silly. Or both."

Bryn sighed. "Probably the latter. But you know Holly. He seems to have a knack for getting out of sticky situations."

"I hope so." Robyn hugged herself. She didn't seem to be able to get warm. "Can you watch the place for a minute? I'm just going up to get a jacket."

"Can I help?" Bryn said, reaching for her as she went past. Just then the first customer of the afternoon walked through the door. She smiled.

"Later," she said, touching his arm.

The afternoon continued to pass slowly. Occasional customers came in but didn't stay long. Bryn went to the outer door a couple of times and said that the street too was very quiet. Most of the time they sat close together behind the counter, their arms around each other, talking quietly. By five they were both beginning to become really concerned about Holly.

"I'm going to close now," Robyn said. "There's been no one in for the last fifty minutes. Then we need to see if we can contact him again."

She locked the front door and replaced the salt barrier, then turned off the fairy lights. As she re-entered the shop and locked the inner door Bryn was busy sending another message to Holly.

"I guess we just keep waiting," he thought aloud.

"Hmm," Robyn said. "I hate waiting."

She began to tidy up the shop, re-shelving some of the books, straightening the scarves, making sure the crystals were all in their correct baskets. The fourth time she started round again Bryn came over and took her hands.

"He's going to be fine," he told her. "And if you tidy any more you're just going to make it untidy again."

"I know," she sighed. "Did I tell you that I hate waiting?"

"You did," he smiled.

"Did I tell you how much?"

"No, but I'm starting to get the picture," he said, pulling her towards him. "Maybe I'd better find a way to take your mind off it for a while."

After a while they went to make toast in the kitchen, even though neither of them were really hungry. Robyn could see the anxiety growing in Bryn's face, despite his efforts to hide it from her.

"He will be OK," she said. "He can't not be."

Bryn gave her a half smile. "I hate the not knowing. Even more than the waiting."

She walked over to where he was sitting to give him a hug. He looked up at her sharply.

"Message," he said. Lifting his t-shirt, they watched the words form on his skin.

"Woods. Help. Trapped."

"Oh no," Robyn gasped. "Holly."

"Come on," Bryn said. They took a moment to load their pockets with salt and old nails and then ran out along the path and straight for the woods. It was surprisingly dark outside, much darker than it should have been. Robyn wished she had brought a torch.

"Holly," Bryn yelled as they got to the trees. "Holly. Where the hell are you?"

"Holly." Robyn added her voice.

They heard a response which seemed not too far to the left.

"Holly, keep talking so we can find you."

"Over here," his voice came back. "To your left, I think. Keep coming. Now look up."

They skidded to a halt and obeyed his instruction. He swung in a net about fifteen feet above their heads.

"Darn," said Bryn. "Is that what I think it is?"

"Yep," said Holly. "And my blade was dropped in the struggle. There weren't that many but they were so strong. I'm lucky they didn't kill me but they've obviously had instructions to keep anyone they take alive. I'd rather not think about why."

"So it must be here somewhere," Bryn said, beginning to search in the undergrowth.

"What are we looking for?" Robyn asked.

"Faerie blade, double edged, silver with a green handle," Bryn said. "It's the only thing that'll cut through those ropes."

"You need to hurry," Holly said. "I know I don't need to tell you this, but they'll be back and I'm pretty sure they'll be bringing reinforcements."

"OK, got the message loud and clear," Bryn said. They hunted and hunted but the knife was nowhere to be found.

"Can you use Holly's magic bottle detector thingy?" Robyn asked.

"We could try," Bryn took it from his pocket. It was already glowing. "It's already picking up quite a lot but it's worth a go."

As he moved around the vicinity, Robyn stood and looked at the tree in which Holly was suspended. It was smooth at the base, the first branch being about eight feet above the ground. After that, she thought, it didn't look too hard to climb. Bryn came back over to stand beside her several minutes later.

"Holly, I can't find it anywhere."

"That's not good," Holly said. "I'm sure it can't be far."

"I know, but it's not here, we've both looked. Maybe there's something back at the shop. Does Julianne have anything that's pure silver and sharp?"

"Probably," Robyn said, thinking hard. "Hang on, ordinary silver but sharp? Or is faerie silver different?"

"Yeah, but not enough to matter. Anything silver will do."

"Don't need to go back then." She held out her arm with the charm bracelet that she usually wore. "It's got an axe, see. Sharper than you'd think. Would that do?"

Bryn hugged her. "You are just full of surprises aren't you? Perfect."

"Hey, lovebirds, I don't want to break up the great romance but would someone kindly get me down?" said Holly, somewhat plaintively.

"Sorry," Bryn said. "Now how...?"

But Robyn was already standing under the lowest branch. "Can you lift me?" she asked. "I think I can climb it if I can just get up there."

Bryn put his arms around her waist and lifted her so she could get a grip of the branch. Then he helped push her upwards until she was able to straddle it.

"OK?" he asked.

"So glad I'm wearing jeans," she muttered to herself. She moved toward the trunk and carefully began to make her way upwards. She fought her way through the twigs and foliage until she reached the level where the net hung.

"Hi," Holly said, looking up at her. "So nice to see you."

"You too," Robyn reciprocated. She looked at the structure of the net. "It looks like if I cut the suspension rope it'll allow the top of the net to open anyway."

"Simple but effective," Holly agreed. Robyn was unsure whether it was a comment on the design of the net or her plan but she set to with the tiny axe anyway and slowly but surely the strands of the rope began to fray and break. She was eighty per cent through when a low eerie sound echoed around them, a deep and chilling cry from a horn calling goodness knows what to it. It was distant but it froze them all to the bone.

"What was that?" Robyn asked, sawing faster and dreading the answer.

"The Wild Hunt," Holly said quietly. "Hurry."

"Almost there. I'm afraid this is going to be a bit of a bump. Bryn, stand clear. Holly, hold tight." The last few strands gave way and the net dropped to the floor.

"Oof," Holly gasped as he landed. Bryn quickly helped him to untangle himself from the net while Robyn scrambled back down to the bottom branch and lowered herself to hang from it. She was about to let go when Bryn caught her round the waist and brought her back down to the ground. The horn sounded again, much closer this time, and they could hear the sound of snarling and barking.

"They're coming," Holly shouted. "Run."

The three of them took off, speeding through the woods as fast as they could. Robyn struggled to keep up with the other two, which they quickly realised; they slowed for her then took a hand each and pulled her along. They careened across the field, down the path and into the garden. Robyn let go and wrestled the key from her pocket but her hands were shaking so hard she couldn't find the keyhole. Holly took it from her and let them in. He locked it behind them.

"We need to check the barriers," Bryn said. He and Robyn took salt and the iron nails and reinforced the blocks across all the openings in the building. Holly was busy checking the charms were all still properly in place. Once done they congregated back in the shop.

"We're safe here for now," Holly said. "They won't be able to get in. But you need to warn the others to stay together and somewhere protected."

Robyn had her phone out. "Done," she said a moment later. "So what now?"

The hunting horn rang out again. It was frighteningly close now.

"They're tracking us aren't they?" Bryn had no doubt in his voice but Holly nodded anyway. There was a ping on Robyn's phone.

"It's from J. "Will do, be careful all of you." What did you find out today, Holly?" Robyn's voice was quiet.

Holly sighed. "Oonagh is healed, but the village and the rest of the court lands are besieged. That was why it took me so long to get back. I had to use a disguise to get through to the border and I wanted to try and pick up some information along the way. I thought I'd got away with it but the goblins had been sent to wait for anyone crossing over who isn't foresworn to Maric."

"They're almost ready to move, aren't they?" Bryn said. Before Holly could answer there was a dreadful noise from the back of the shop, snapping, snarling, howling and the sound of splintering wood. Running into the kitchen, they were horrified by the sight in front of them.

The back garden was teeming with massive black hounds, thickset and muscular with burning red eyes. Behind them were three of the biggest horses Robyn had ever seen, their hooves causing whirlwinds of dust as they circled restlessly. The large figures astride them seemed to fixate menacingly on the door, even though their faces were hidden. The back fence lay in shards beneath them.

"Pull the blinds down," Bryn ordered. They shaded all the windows they could, upstairs and down.

"Bring the crystals down with you, Robyn," Holly said. Robyn's heart lurched and her gut twisted into knots, but she retrieved the crystals from the box. Putting the pendulum around her neck she went back down into the shop.

"You never got a chance to answer Bryn's question, did you Holly?" she said.

"No," Holly replied. "But he's not wrong. They're coming sooner that we thought. The lunar eclipse was a distraction, a possibility that was nurtured and grown by Maric's side to mislead us. All of us."

"So what's happening? When? Holly, what did you find out?"

"There's a New Moon tonight," Holly said. He looked up at the clock. "It's the time of greatest darkness, the lowest energy for the shield. That's when they will be coming through, Maric and all his forces. That's why there are so many of the Wild Hunt here, so many hounds. To besiege you and stop you from healing the void."

"With what?" Robyn snapped with more anger than she felt. She slammed the three crystals down on the counter. "I don't know which one it is. Hell, it might not be any of them. It could be still out there somewhere. I just don't know."

Bryn put his arm around her. "It's going to be OK."

"You'll know which one when you need to." Holly tried to be reassuring, but Robyn gave them both a withering stare. She left Bryn's arm where it was though.

"Oh, really? That sounds like such crap I don't even think you believe it. How on earth is it going to be OK? We're surrounded by venomous hounds, homicidal huntsmen and goodness only knows what else. It's pitch black out there and I don't know if I've even found the missing piece, even if we could, by some miracle, get where we need to be, wherever that is. And we're nearly out of time. How is that even remotely near OK?" She heard the hysterical edge to her voice and hated herself for it.

"There must be a way," Bryn said. "We just have to find it."

"I think you need to get to the cliffs," Holly ventured after a moment. "Where land and sea meet, it makes sense. It's a junction. Makes the barrier easier to cross, especially when there's a lot..." His voice faded.

"How can we get there and avoid the demon dogs? The fields are too open, they'd pick us off long before we got anywhere near," Bryn said.

Robyn swallowed nervously. She had an idea but it frightened her almost as much as the hounds. "The tunnels," she whispered.

She heard Bryn's sharp intake of breath. Holly stared at her, his expression a mixture of consternation and admiration. "Too risky," he said. "You could be lost, or worse." But Robyn could see in his eyes that behind the concern he was weighing up the idea. She took a deep breath.

"I don't think we have a choice. It'll all be lost anyway. We... I have to try. Or has anyone got a better plan?"

The silence that followed hung heavy over the three of them.

"I'll take that as a no then," Robyn said eventually. She picked up the crystals, slipping them into the pocket of her jeans. Checking that the tiger's eye was still in place on its cord round her neck, she swung her black jacket on and grabbed a torch from under the counter. "Right."

"I'm coming with you," Bryn told her.

"No, you can't. It's too dangerous."

"Exactly. That's why I'm not going to let you go alone."

"He's right," said Holly. "I'll stay and do what I can here to distract them."

"I don't suppose you can make us invisible?" Robyn joked half-heartedly.

"Unfortunately not, but I can create a glamour to draw them away. Fifteen, twenty minutes at most and then they'll realise and come back, but at least it will give you a head start."

"Thanks." Robyn and Bryn walked out into the kitchen and stuffed more salt into their pockets. Holly followed them, standing in the doorway. In the darkness they could barely see each other.

"Good luck," Holly said. "Wait until you hear the motorbike. It should give you time to get to the entrance and a little way through at least."

"Be safe," Robyn told him. Bryn raised his hand as Holly went back into the shop.

Chapter 17

THEY positioned themselves on either side of the back door. Bryn pulled the blind forward very slightly and peered out. He could just make out the seething mass of hound bodies that filled the garden, the glowing red of their eyes and the occasional flash of teeth. Their low growling was eerie and constant. He glanced over at Robyn, her face a pale shadow in the almost non-existent light. She was pressed against the doorpost with her eyes shut. He was about to reach for her hand when everything suddenly fell silent. The dogs stilled, turning toward the road. Then they heard the unmistakeable roar of his bike passing in front of the shop and the low clear call of the Hunters' horn. As if one creature, the hounds streamed away along the drive to the street, baying for blood.

"How, what...?" Robyn was astounded but Bryn had the door open and they were already running for the woods.

"Holly's glamoured us as a decoy but he can't sustain it long. We have to hurry."

They flew across the fields and through the trees, straining to see in the minimal light, and hurled themselves through the split in the tree trunk into the cave below. Robyn flicked on her torch, salt ready in her other hand, but the chamber was empty.

"OK then."

They headed down into the tunnels. The first few choices were relatively easy as the passages were short and they both remembered the same turns from when they had followed Silver. Then they found themselves in a cavern with five exits and stopped abruptly.

"Which one, which one?" Robyn whispered desperately, turning full circle. Bryn shone his torch down each tunnel.

"I don't know," he said finally. "They all look the same."

Robyn felt the panic reaching up to choke her. "What are we going to do?"

Bryn put his hands on her shoulders and made her look at him. "You can find the way. That's why you're here. Trust yourself. You know. So breathe. Close your eyes and breathe and the answer will be there."

Robyn felt like screaming at him or hitting him or something for acting so calm, but it seemed totally pointless so she just did as he said. She leaned her head against him and actually, as her breathing slowed and the panic receded she became aware of her guide; the rushing, soothing pulse of the sea. Breaking away from Bryn's grip she listened carefully at the mouth of each tunnel until she could hear the sound most clearly.

"The sea," she said. "This way." And they were off again.

They raced on, listening over the rasp of their breath for the sea and for signs of pursuit. The tunnel had occasional openings on either side which they ignored, heading for the waves.

"Must be near," Bryn said as the tunnel began to narrow.

"How would we know?" Robyn commented. "These tunnels twist and turn and run round each other. It's a maze and we're running blind."

"There's a change up ahead," Bryn said confidently, shining his torch as far forward as he could. "Maybe it's the cave that opens onto the cliff." His hopes were dashed a moment later when the passage spat them out into another cavern with multiple openings.

"Oh, no," Robyn groaned. She tried listening at each opening, then looked at Bryn in despair. "They all sound the same."

Bryn looked around. "There has to be a way."

Robyn stood still and tried to calm herself. "Think, think," she muttered, clutching the pendulum at her throat. "Maybe I could dowse but that would take too long. But it might be the only way." She shook her hand to ease an itch, realising when it failed to abate that it was actually more of a tickle. Looking down she saw a spider balanced on her middle finger. She moved her hand again but the spider stayed put. "That's weird," she thought. "They usually run." She brought her hand up for a closer look and the spider seemed to stare back at her. It was silvery green and had a definite glow around it.

"Bryn, come and look at..."

There was a sound from behind them, faint but unmistakeable, echoing through the tunnels. The Hunt had picked up their trail.

"Decision time," said Bryn grimly.

"Bryn, look." The spider had slowly but purposefully moved to the end of Robyn's finger and dropped down to the floor on a thread that gleamed in the torch light. She ran across to the cave wall and took off down one of the tunnels. The silk trail was clearly visible.

"Whoa. That's not the one you rescued, surely?" Bryn sounded incredulous.

"I don't know, but it doesn't matter. Come on."

They plunged after the spider, following the sparkling strand into the dark. As they moved they became aware of streams on the walls either side of them moving back the way they had come. The weak beams from the torches showed hundreds of spiders collecting at the entrance and weaving a strong silken block to the tunnel. It was already obscuring half the opening.

"Wow."

"Thanks," Robyn gasped, breathless with the breakneck pace. They followed their guide up and down and round, sure footed now through the confusing network of the tunnels. The spider slowed slightly when the angry baying became howls of fury, and then speeded up. The hounds had obviously reached the block.

"It'll take a while for them to get through," Robyn thought but she had no breath to speak.

Gradually they began to notice a change in the air, less mossy earthiness and more salt tang. Eventually they came out under the overhang by the path, on the level below the main cave entrance. They snapped their torches off so as not to be seen. The spider silk still glistened and shone, amplified now in the small amount of light from the sliver of moon. As Robyn looked across the sea she felt a jolt of recognition. She had been here so many times in her dreams. She held her hand up to the spider in gratitude.

"Thank you so much. You and the others." The creature bobbed in reply, then turned and ran back into the caves.

The howling of the pack was slowly getting closer. "Come on," urged Bryn. "While we still have half a chance."

Staying close to the rock face and using any other cover they could find, they made their way as quickly and quietly as possible up toward the cliff top. As they climbed they noticed the wind building in power, the air thickening around them. Peering around the boulder at the top of the path, they struggled to pick anything out.

"Doesn't seem to be anything up here," said Bryn.

"Yet." Robyn didn't need to add the word. They both knew what was coming. She strained her eyes, trying to make out something, anything in the dark. All she could see was the thinnest ribbon of silver light on the sea.

"Oh," she gasped, moving toward it. Bryn tried to pull her back but she resisted. "This is right, I'm sure of it." She drew him forward. "Look, over there."

They walked carefully toward the reflecting light, wary to stay well away from the edge of the cliff.

"What do you think will...?" Robyn began to ask, but at that moment they both stopped, watching in horror as great clouds of shadow swept across the sky, blotting out the few faint stars that had been visible and seeming to suck away the little light coming from the moon. As the shadows began to coalesce the wind increased, whipping their faces and screaming like a train at full speed. The writhing black mass grew into a monstrous tower, all the while coming towards them and the centre began to spin, faster and faster until it seemed to tear itself apart. A circular void formed in the middle and began to expand, letting out a dull glow. Shapes and figures became apparent, restless, urging forward, desperate to break through. The roiling mass was almost on them now, so close to the cliff that it was almost touching.

"Now, Robyn," Bryn yelled. "Throw it."

Robyn dug trembling hands into her pocket, yanking out the crystals. "Which one?" she cried.

"Doesn't matter. One at a time 'til it works."

The wind was deafening and so powerful that Robyn could barely move against it. She forced herself forward slightly and hurled the jasper with all her might. Nothing. The gap was widening faster now, the acceleration terrifying. She threw the crystal point. Still no change.

"The dogs," Bryn shouted. "Hurry."

Robyn could hear them even over the wind. She threw the piece of agate into the gaping hole. Still nothing. "I've failed," she thought miserably. "Some hero." The swirling hole just kept growing and Robyn could see the figures clearly now, straining forward, some beginning to emerge; a serpent with wings and emerald fangs, wraith-like masses of dark mist, a massive arm attached to an even bigger torso.

Bryn came over to her. He was speaking but the wind stole his words. He put his hand to his throat. She finally understood and tore off the tiger's eye, flinging it frantically into the vortex. It made no difference at all. She dropped to her knees in disbelief, crushed that everything they had gone through, fought for, had been for nothing. She felt Bryn's hand on her shoulder, heard him say - or did she just think she heard it - "You couldn't have done any more." Then she felt him jerk away from her. Turning, she realised that the dogs had finally caught up with them, pouring around them in a hellish mass of snapping teeth and red eyes. Bryn was trying to hold them off with a fallen branch, but she could see that he would soon be overwhelmed.

"No."

The shout was torn from her by some unknown strength that she hadn't known she possessed. She stood up and glared at the spinning horror in front of her. More of the creatures were part way through now, huge four legged beasts with other beasts as riders, broad metal clad figures with fierce looking weaponry. And then, in the centre, gliding through the rest to pause at the front, a tall hooded figure emanating a chilling, dark aura of power. Robyn could feel the constriction round her throat without him having to do anything, the heavy crushing weight around her lungs which his mere presence seemed to induce. There was no mistaking who that was and, as he swept his hands apart, seeming to open the gap effortlessly, somehow she didn't care, wasn't afraid any more. He moved right into the veil of what remained of the shield and raised his hand toward her. Just standing still against him was like trying to stop an articulated lorry, but she was overwhelmed by a fury that she didn't know she was capable of.

"No." The scream ripped out of her again over the roaring wind as she saw Bryn go down amongst the hounds. "You can't have this world. Or the Faerie realm. And you can't have him." And almost before she knew what she was doing she was running, leaping, launching herself and flying straight at Maric into the middle of the void.

There was a blinding flash. An ear splitting explosion. The earth itself seemed to shudder. And then there was silence.

When Robyn came to, slowly and painfully, dawn was softening the sky, a gentle wash of lavender streaked with crimson. Bryn was sitting with his back against one of the boulders, cradling her against him. A short distance away, closer to the edge of the cliff, Holly sat cross legged on the grass playing his wooden pipe. The notes bubbled over to her on the breeze, cascading over the rushing sigh of the sea.

Robyn tried to sit up and immediately slumped back against Bryn, head thumping. He looked down at her face, relief replacing the mask of worry.

"Thank goodness," he said. "I was scared you were never going to wake up. Holly said you'd be OK but I had my doubts. He didn't see..."

Robyn tried to move again and gave up. "Ow."

"I should think so," Bryn agreed. A smile hovered around his lips, but his eyes were still full of concern. "Just stay still and rest. You deserve it."

"We're still here," Robyn whispered. "But I was wrong. About the crystals. They didn't do anything. What happened?"

"You happened." Now Bryn couldn't stop himself from smiling broadly, even though he was shaking his head at the memory. "You healed the rip. Scared me half to death in the process but hey. You did it."

"How? I don't understand."

"Neither do I. Do you remember anything?"

"Just black, swirling clouds and wind, feeling desperate and the dogs nearly killing you. And anger. And then nothing. Did you see what happened?"

Bryn cradled her head as he altered his position so he could see her better.

"I was almost drowning in that pack of dogs and I could see two of the huntsmen coming across the top. I looked round to try and warn you and there you were taking a flying leap right into the middle of that black hole. You vanished right into it and there was an almighty explosion which knocked me off my feet. I must've hit my head because when I came to the stars were out properly and everything was quiet. No vortex, no dogs, no gale, just quiet. And then I saw you lying on the grass, so still, and I thought..." He stopped, his eyes clouding. "But when I got to you, you were breathing OK, so I just sat with you." He trailed off.

"So... it's OK? The veil's sealed?"

"Yeah. Holly knew you'd managed to fix it before he got here. But when I explained how, I think that was a surprise."

"How could I do it? We didn't have the missing piece."

"Yes we did. We had it all along, we just didn't realise it. You are... were the missing piece. Or some part of you was. Because none of us knew what we were looking for, we assumed it would be a physical thing, an artefact of some kind. But clearly it was you."

Robyn looked up at him. A thousand questions ran through her head but she didn't have the energy to ask them. Bryn stroked her hair gently and without the need for her to ask, confirmed what was important.

"We're all still here and the world's OK. Both of them, because of you. Now rest."

Robyn awoke later to the sound of quiet conversation. Julianne and Fiona had come to find them after Bryn had texted to say where they were. The sun was warm and for the first time in weeks the sky was a strong cloudless blue. She moved cautiously but the thump in her head had dissipated to a dull ache.

"Hey," said Bryn. He helped her to sit up. "How are you?"

"Better thanks. Hi guys."

"Hi yourself," said Fiona. "It's very good to see you, and in pretty much one piece too."

"I hear you nearly gave Bryn a heart attack," Julianne admonished her gently. "Next time you throw yourself off a cliff into a mass of evil beings, perhaps you should warn innocent bystanders first."

Robyn laughed and then winced. "Don't worry, I'm not planning on doing it again any time soon." Her voice was hoarse.

"Here," Holly said. "Take some of this." He pulled a small flask from his belt. Bryn reached for it and passed it over to her. She drank deeply. The liquid tasted of honey and herbs and spread like light through her body, calming and soothing her.

"Wow," she said. "That's amazing. Thanks."

"I think you're the one who deserves thanks," Holly said. "From everyone. You saved us all."

Chapter 18

THEY sat for a little longer and then made their way slowly back to the shop. Jim was waiting for them with Oonagh and a man none of them except Holly recognised.

"I'm so relieved to see you three," Jim said to Robyn and Bryn. "I knew you were OK when we got Bryn's text but even so."

Robyn hugged him. "We're fine. Just a bit bruised and tired, that's all."

"Come and sit." He had brought chairs and stools in for all of them and the little kitchen was crowded.

"We owe you a huge debt," said Oonagh. "You have all taken enormous risks and the three of you," she looked at Robyn, Holly and Bryn, "took the biggest risk of all yesterday. You knew you could so easily have been lost and yet you still went out and saved us anyway."

"Indeed," the man agreed. "I am Rayner, another of the circle of elders. I think that we can never repay you fully but we can extend our gratitude."

"It was our world as well," said Bryn. "And we couldn't have got there if it weren't for the help you gave us."

"Without your magical protection and guidance, we surely would have been lost," Robyn added.

"We know what happened here," Fiona said. "What happened on your side?"

"We were under attack during the evening," Rayner replied. "The Ashling Court was besieged from early in the afternoon, but the ferocity of the onslaught intensified later. I believe it was to engage us and prevent us from going to the borders, to the breach. Eventually it became very dark and there was an almighty explosion which seemed to make even the rocks shake. It knocked most of us to the ground. When we recovered, the enemy was in disarray, most fleeing back to the hills. Our soldiers went out and caught many of them."

"Did you get Maric? And his creepy sidekicks?" Robyn asked. Holly grinned at the description, but Oonagh answered seriously.

"Yes. He was seriously weakened by what you did. We also captured three of his inner circle. The remaining one will be found soon, I am confident of that. They are safely contained where their sorcery will not be a problem."

"That's a relief," Julianne and Fiona said together.

"I still don't understand how the rift was healed," Robyn said.

"That is a mystery," Rayner agreed. "When the shield fragmented eighteen years ago and the piece was lost, it should have been easy to trace."

"Especially since it was lost here," Oonagh added. "But it disappeared so quickly and has been impossible to find. It's only in the last few years that it seems to have been centred here in the Dragon's Rest."

"That's why we thought you were probably involved Robyn, it coincides with when you started coming in here," Fiona said.

"But it doesn't explain why it was Robyn who fixed it," Holly said.

But a sudden realisation came to Robyn then and her hands flew to her mouth. "Oh," she gasped.

They all turned to stare at her.

"Are you OK?" Jim asked.

"Do you know exactly when it was lost?" Robyn asked the elders.

"Around the summer solstice," Oonagh said.

"Around my birthday."

"Why does that make a difference? You live miles away," Julianne said.

"Yes, but I was born here, in the village. I didn't even think about it before. First week of Mum's maternity leave, they came down for a long weekend and I decided to make an early appearance. Scuppered their plans completely, but it kind of fits with what you said. We were whizzed off to hospital and then obviously went home. So if for some reason the fragment attached itself to me that would be why you couldn't find it here."

"Well. That would explain a few things," Holly said.

"It's most unexpected but it seems to make sense," Rayner agreed.

Julianne opened her mouth and then shut it again. Jim laughed.

"Speaking of unexpected and unusual things, I think you've actually managed to render Julianne speechless."

"Cheek," Julianne spluttered, and they all laughed.

"We must go now," Oonagh said. "But again, thank you. All is as it should be again and that is the best way for both worlds."

The two faeries left and walked away together towards what was left of the back fence. There was a slight shimmer in the air and they disappeared.

"Oh," said Robyn. Despite all she had seen, she still couldn't quite believe it.

"OK," said Jim. "Nobody got any sleep last night, and being knocked unconscious doesn't count Robyn, before you say anything. You three look positively shattered. So I am going to serve up a big breakfast and then we are all going to get some rest."

"But what about...?" Robyn began.

"The shop is staying closed today," Julianne said. "And although there's no risk now I would really like it if you would all come back to ours and sleep. We've got sleeping bags and bedrolls. You may think it's daft but I just want everyone together for a bit."

Robyn reached across and hugged her. "I'd love to," she said.

They walked through the village all together, seeing how the warmth and clear sunshine had brought so many people out.

"So different from yesterday," Bryn observed.

"They don't know how lucky they are," Fiona said, linking her good arm through Robyn's. "Look at them. Not a clue."

"Best it stays that way." Holly wore his usual mischievous grin, but his eyes were serious.

After Jim's big breakfast and a further catch up, Julianne sorted out bedrolls and sleeping bags and pillows for her visitors. They rearranged the furniture in the sitting room to make space and pulled the thick curtains to block out the light.

"I've been to parties that have ended like this," Bryn said.

"Well, if they started anything like last night, I'm glad I haven't." Fiona was laughing. "Right, I'm going to try and get some sleep because I am pooped." She clambered into the nearest sleeping bag. Holly looked at the other two and grinned.

"Guess I'll take this one," he said, settling into the one next to Fiona.

Robyn and Bryn took the two at the end. "You did it," he whispered as he pulled her close.

"We did it," she replied. She buried her head against his chest and closed her eyes. "Thank goodness."

They didn't surface until late afternoon, and even then realised that they were still exhausted. Robyn felt bruised and sore and Fiona couldn't stop yawning. They said goodbye and headed out to their respective homes. Bryn and Holly walked back with Robyn to the shop. Holly hugged Robyn tightly.

"You're extraordinary, prophecy girl," he said. "No more doubts about yourself in that head I hope."

She smiled at him. "I think we're all pretty amazing."

"Very true," he said. "I'll see you soon."

They watched him walk back up to the main street. "Where does he go?" Robyn wondered.

"Oh, he's got lots of places to stay," Bryn said. "He's a bit like a stray cat. Can always find a welcome somewhere. Plenty of people are pleased to see Holly, especially the girls." He grinned. "Now you go and sleep some more, and I'll go back and see my parents before they forget what I look like. See you tomorrow."

She reached up to kiss him, and then he kissed her some more. When she finally went inside she was glowing. The Dragon's Rest was peaceful, a lightness in the air replacing the heavy magical energy that had been there before. Robyn took some delight in wandering around the shop and enjoying the sense of relief that she felt. It was a while before she headed upstairs to have a long soak in the bath and fall into bed.

Robyn slept late the following morning and had only just got downstairs when Julianne came in.

"Sorry," she said. "My nightmare alarm clock has finally stopped. Now I'm late."

"You don't have to apologise for anything. I wouldn't blame you if you needed to sleep for a week. Anyway, you're not working today. There's something else that's lined up for you."

"J, I am working today. You've had to cover for me a lot. There's not much point me coming down here to help if I don't do my share."

"Yes, well, I suppose you haven't had anything more important to do like, oh I don't know, saving humanity, have you? Just been out gallivanting the whole time."

Robyn shrugged. "Still."

"Nope. You are going out today. Bryn asked me last night if you could have time off to go somewhere with him and of course I said yes." She looked coyly at Robyn. "Unless of course you don't want to."

But Robyn was already smiling. "Really?"

"Yes really. And I think you might finally get to ride on that motorbike, so I'd wear jeans if I were you. He said he'd come by for you but that you were welcome to go over to the hall if you wanted. He's got his class this morning."

"J, are you sure?"

"Go on, go and get changed. That skirt is way too long to be safe on a bike."

Robyn put on black jeans and a black top and picked up her leather jacket. She sat in the shop with Julianne for a bit but found it difficult to settle. She decided to wander over to the hall at about quarter to eleven, hoping that the walk would calm the butterflies in her stomach. After all they had been through, she didn't understand why she felt so nervous about seeing Bryn.

She slipped quietly into the hall and stood near the door, watching. Bryn had his back to her and was playing a bass line while the kids were playing chords and harmonies over the top. It sounded really good and she applauded enthusiastically when they finished. Bryn turned round and the look of delight on his face when he saw her almost took her breath away.

"Hey, it's Robyn," said Mallory. "Are you going to play?"

Bryn beckoned her over. "That sounded great, guys," he said.

"Maybe but I'd really like to listen. Got any others I can hear?" Robyn asked the kids. There were some enthusiastic suggestions, and Bryn got them to do an impromptu performance of the three songs they had been working on.

"You lot are amazing," Robyn said as they left. "Let me know when you play your first gig. I want front row tickets." She unplugged Bryn's guitar and amp and began to wind leads while he saw them out, but he took them out of her hands when he returned so he could kiss her.

"I missed you," he said. "But I've got you for the whole day today haven't I? Goblin free."

She nodded against him. They loaded his stuff into the car and took it back to his parents" place. Then he retrieved a box from the kitchen and helmets and gloves for them both.

"Are you happy to go on the bike?" he asked.

She nodded. "Never been on one before though."

"Just hang on and move with it. You can hold on to the bar at the back." He smiled at her. "But I'd rather you held on to me."

He helped her fasten the helmet and she slipped onto the bike behind him. The low roar of the engine kicked in and she slid her arms round Bryn's waist as they took off. As he drove she rested her head against his back and watched the world passing by. It was a feeling of complete freedom and it blew her away. He drove for quite a while, away into the wild green spaces of the southern tip of Cornwall. When they stopped they were near to the Lizard, in a quiet place high over the sea.

"That was incredible," Robyn enthused once they had removed their helmets. "And this place, it's so beautiful."

"It's one of my favourite places to be," Bryn said. He took a blanket from the storage space at the back of the bike, and spread it on the ground. "I wanted you to see it. Here, I made us a picnic."

They sat and ate and talked and laughed. Then they went walking through the green, enjoying the sunshine and being together. As the sun began to dip they wandered back to the bike and Bryn drove them into one of the smaller towns along the way.

"Have dinner with me too?" he asked.

They went to a little Italian place to eat. Bryn insisted on paying as well, despite Robyn's attempts to do so.

"I'll give you money for petrol then," she said.

"No, you won't," he demurred. "Today is on me."

"Why, though?" Robyn asked. They were walking back but he stopped and put his arms round her.

"Because I want you to know how special you are. And how you deserve to be treated." His lips brushed her forehead. "And I want to prove to you that all guys aren't like that idiot two timer who didn't know what he had."

"I know that," she whispered into his shoulder.

It was ten before they got back to the Dragon's Rest and Bryn as usual walked her to the door. She unlocked it and sighed.

"It's weird, you know," she said. "Not dreading going to sleep because of the dreams, not having to salt the doors and windows, having time to chill out rather than running around in a panic all the time because the world's about to come tumbling down."

"It's good though." Bryn moved closer to her. "Isn't it?"

"Not sure what I'll do for the next hour or so," she said shyly. "I don't suppose you want to come in for a while and distract me, do you?"

The smile he gave her and the look in his eyes was all the answer she needed.

About The Author

IZZY used to work in the medical field in London and following a huge downshift, now works as a complementary therapist, author and editor based in a quiet village in Dorset. She has developed her portfolio over the past couple of years and indulges her writing with ethereal passion.

She writes about her love of the unusual and magical with stories predominantly aimed at young adults and the young at heart. "Maybe I never really grew up" she says. "I love the idea that anything is possible. Someone once told me that magic isn't all whizz-bang theatrics, it's the occurrence of the unexpected. We just have to open our eyes and look."

Visit IzzyRobertsonAuthor.co.uk for further details.

Children from the Kundeni School planting trees

Be Part of the Magic Oxygen Word Forest

As well as delivering great content to our readers, we are also the home of the Magic Oxygen Literary Prize.

It is a global writing competition like no other, as we plant a tree for every entry in our tropical Word Forest. We publish the shortlist and winners in an anthology and plant an additional tree for every copy sold.

The forest is situated beside the Kundeni School in Bore, Kenya, a remote community that has suffered greatly from deforestation. Trees planted near the equator are the most efficient at capturing carbon from the atmosphere - 250kg per tree - and keeping our planet cool. The forest will also reintroduce biodiversity and provide food and income for the community.

Visit MagicOxygen.co.uk to buy the anthology and find out about the next MOLP, then spread news of it far and wide on your blogs and social media and be part of a pioneering literary legacy.

Visit CarbonLink.org for updates on our project.